I0588625

in case of emergency press

We are proud to acknowledge the Traditional Owners of
country throughout Australia and to recognise their
continuing connection to land, waters, and culture.
We pay our respects to their Elders.

We support recognition, reconciliation, and reparation.

Killing Justice

Phil Copsey

in case of emergency press
https://icoe.com.au
Travancore, Victoria
Australia

Published by in case of emergency press 2023

ISBN: 978-0-6458496-2-2

Cover design: Steph Babinczky

Acknowledgements

To Steph Babinczky. The most amazing cover designer!

Dedication

To Liz.
Enough said.

Table of Contents

Killing Justice

Phil Copsey

Chapter 1

Bogdan Vulpe sat in the back pew of the Victorian Supreme Court in William Street, Melbourne. He was not there because he was interested in law or how the court system in the state of Victoria functioned. He was there because he wanted to see the face of the judge who had dared to ignore his wishes. Not actual wishes, more directives in fact.

He observed The Right Honourable Miles Wilson, decked out in his full-length robe with the three red stripes on his sleeves, sitting in his chair high above the rest of the legal fraternity scattered around on the floor of the court below him.

The sentence was about to be handed down on one of Australia's biggest drug couriers, and at any other time, and in any other place, Vulpe would not have cared less about the fate of the accused drug runner and dealer by the name of Chiril Cel Tradat. However, on this occasion, the man about to be sentenced was Vulpe's main organiser.

Cel Tradat looked from the prisoner's dock down at his embattled barrister, then across to the prosecution bench where another barrister was sitting with his legs crossed, turned to one side. He was conducting a friendly conversation with the Detective Sergeant who had arrested and subsequently charged Cel Tradat with possession of the huge trafficable amount of pure grade heroin that had been found in a Collingwood factory some months before.

The accused had not worried at all about being charged because he knew that his boss, Bogdan Vulpe would never let him go to gaol. Money would change hands with the police, or the judiciary and he would either be given bail, by where he could skip the country quite easily or, if he had to sit in Barwon State prison for a while, he knew that if he went to court, he would be found not guilty on all charges. He was now sweating on the second outcome. When the foreman of the jury had returned with a guilty verdict he was taken back, but at the same time he believed His Honour would hand down a short term of imprisonment. Vulpe would have seen that money had crossed the judge's palm to affect that result. The one thing he felt a little uneasy with was the way Vulpe was avoiding his confident look. His attention was quickly drawn back to the present when he heard the judge's call for silence in the court so the sentence could be handed down.

Cel Tradat heard the sentence of twenty years being delivered by Judge Miles Wilson but he did not hear the clicking sound of the steel manacles that the custody officers standing directly behind made as they quickly handcuffed and spun him around. They then pulled him towards the downwards leading staircase at the back of the dock. That staircase only ended at one place and that was the cells of the Supreme Court. A short wait there, then the long trip in the back of a prison van down the Geelong Road to his new place of abode was all he could look forward to.

This wasn't happening, was all Cel Tradat could think.

People would answer for this, was all Vulpe could think as he rose and stormed from the court.

Chapter 2

Vulpe sat in the upstairs office of 342 Nicholson Street, the corporate premises of the Cleanstyle Industrial Cleaning Company. It was one of several legitimate businesses that he owned along with a carpet warehouse and a chain of lighting shops. He had placed several relatives in charge of them and had them send detailed profit and loss statements to one of his crime lieutenants every month for scrupulous forensic accounting. No one dared skim anything from these businesses in fear of retribution via a visit from one of Vulpe's heavies. And there was plenty that might have been skimmed. Cleanstyle held some very large government contracts, both state and federal for the maintenance of not only Number One Treasury Place, the headquarters of the Victorian State Premier, but also Number Four Treasury Place, the Melbourne Office of the Prime Minister.

Vulpe had called a meeting of his crime lieutenants, Codrin Dalca and Anton Funan. Vulpe was past the furious stage. He wanted answers and he wanted them now.

He turned from looking out of the large window in front of him and spoke with steel in his voice towards the two sweating thugs.

"I now have two situations that need fixing. One is the fact that my man has been sentenced to twenty years in prison and the second is that you both failed to convince that judge to find some way of declaring a mistrial and letting Cel Tradat go free. Through your negligence you have sentenced Cel Tradat to death within the walls of Barwon State prison. I cannot have him talking to anybody about my business dealings seeing that he is the only other person besides myself that knows all about my life both in the legitimate form and the other more profitable form. I will handle this, but I want full explanations from you two as to why you could not convince this Miles Wilson character to see it our way. I presume you did offer him the one hundred thousand dollars that we talked about?"

Dalca answered his employer with a hesitant voice. "Boss, we thought we had him a couple of days ago. We tailed and got to him at a restaurant in St. Kilda. As he pulled up in his Merc, we had words with him in front of his wife. She was terrified but he didn't say anything. I told him straight to his face that the one hundred thousand was his in cash. Direct swap for finding something wrong in the evidence of that cop Tyler from Melbourne CIU. He knew it would be in his best interest to cooperate. He nodded his head like he would go along with everything. Even told his missus to go inside to the restaurant. He quietly told me and Anton that it had to be done after the case."

"What happened after that?" Vulpe said as he stepped up to Dalca's face.

"He just nodded and walked away when I said the cash would be in his car down in the underground car park of the court when Cel Tradat walked free. I waited down there out of sight and Anton phoned me to say he got twenty years. I was still standing there behind a pillar ten minutes later when that judge came down and got into his car. He had four big fucking coppers with him, and I know two of them are with Major Crime. I waited till he drove out with the heavies who followed him in a four-wheel drive."

Vulpe stared from Dalca to Funan and back again. He knew he had been told the truth because he had seen the four suits get up immediately from their vantage points around the court and make their way outside. Wilson had obviously gone straight to the police after he had been threatened. He had to think. First things first though.

"Both of you get out of my sight now. You had better think seriously about the fact you have let me down. I now must take a step I didn't want to take. Revenge. You two will get that for me. This judge must learn that I will not be ignored. In the meantime Dalca, get our person at the prison to contact me. There must be one less prisoner at morning roll call in a couple of days' time."

Codrin Dalca and Anton Funan exited the office very quickly giving each other nervous looks. Dalca reached into his pocket for his phone and pressed the code name for their prison contact—*The Geelong Cleaner*. When the call was picked up, he spoke.

"The boss needs to speak to you about a mutual friend of ours. Ring him in ten minutes."

The *Geelong Cleaner* sat down and looked at the clock on her kitchen wall and then the photo of her daughter next to the phone. She thought to herself that she would never be rid of the old country and its ways. No matter where you moved to, you were Romanian all your life.

Elena Rosu had managed to escape the old ways and her violent husband and make a new life for herself in her adopted country of Australia. She was a cook by trade and had worked in several hotel kitchens on the Bellarine Peninsula near her hometown of Geelong to support herself and nine-year-old daughter Anna. With the COVID pandemic though, restaurants had shut one after the other so when she saw a government advertisement in the Geelong Advertiser for a senior cook at Barwon State prison, she applied immediately. To her surprise she had been given the position where she now ran the day-to-day supply of meals to all the prisoners. Everything had been going well until one of the inmates, an old Romanian con man had recognised her serving food and had made a call to Vulpe in exchange for a job when he got released in two years.

Vulpe had Rosu tracked to her house and then some days later had paid her a visit after hours. A quick explanation that she either did his bidding from time to time inside the walls of Barwon State prison or Rosu's family back in Romania would suffer, quickly convinced her to go along. Some passing of messages back and forth was a small price to pay for her family's safety. After months with no contact, she had almost forgotten Bogdan Vulpe. He however had not forgotten the hold he had on her.

After a few minutes, Rosu picked up her phone and hesitatingly rang Vulpe.

"You wanted to speak to me?" she said with trepidation in her voice.

"Elena, I will ring you back immediately on another phone," Vulpe said.

Within fifteen seconds, Rosu's mobile rang. No number came up on her screen.

"Yes," Rosu said quietly into her phone wondering why she was now receiving a call from a silent number.

"Elena, I have a job for you. A little more than passing some information back and forth but this is important, and before you answer, think of the consequences to your Romanian family back home."

Fear sent a shiver up Rosu's spine as she listened to Vulpe.

"What is it?"

"You have an inmate at your prison by the name of Chiril Cel Tradat. Within two days this man must be dead. I'm sure with your capabilities as head chef you can arrange a final meal for him. Tasty but deadly!"

Rosu's hand began to shake as she stuttered into the phone. "No, no. I won't," she said loudly in reply.

"I believe you have a six-year-old nephew by the name of Stefan who lives in Rimetea in the old country," Vulpe said with a voice of steel. "If you want him to see his seventh birthday then you will go along with what I want. You will receive a delivery of a small vial. The contents must go into Cel's meal. Understand?"

Rosu replied in a shaking, scared voice, "Yes, I understand."

"Remember this. I know where you live and I can reach your family any time I want. Do not cross me." The line went dead.

Rosu dropped her phone and burst into tears.

Chapter 3

The middle of the low, round coffee table was decorated with a ceramic tray containing pebbles of different colours and four small glass containers holding candles, of which none were lit. It made the table look like somewhere you could sit around and hold a very pleasant conversation while sipping a weak soy latte. Very relaxing.

The other side of the table nearest to the large office desk had several coffee table style books all depicting things pertinent to the Victoria Police, from its history, which was the smallest book, to one entitled, *The Modern Day Police Officer and Community Policing*, which showed the cover picture of the female Inspector in the uniform of the London Metropolitan Police Service in whose office both Senior Sergeant Tony Signorotto, the Officer in Charge of the Carlton police station, and his sub-charge Senior Sergeant Kate McLaren, were now sitting. They had been shown into Superintendent Anne Reid's domain some ten minutes before and told to wait.

Tony Signorotto was quite okay with waiting. After all, he was getting paid to sit in the austere office and look out of the window of the thirty-fifth floor of 311 Spencer Street, the new ultra-modern police headquarters. His offsider, however, was starting to get a little annoyed. Kate McLaren looked first at the closed door and then at the smiling face of Signorotto.

"She's playing power games. It's all about who's running the show. Phil Stone would never have done this to anyone. I bet you she's out there chatting to one of the Assistant Commissioners," an increasingly angry McLaren said.

The reference to their retired Superintendent Phil Stone,

made Signorotto smile even wider. "I'll tell him that tonight when I'm having a beer with him down at the Sarah Sands. We're catching up for a meal. You're not the only one who can spot the games you know. It'll be interesting to meet her. She came into the job sideways from an Inspector's position in the Met in London. A bit of an expert on community policing in ethnic communities, I've been told. Let's not judge a book by its cover, eh Kate?" Signorotto said pointing to the coffee table and having a quiet laugh at the same time.

"If she wants to see community policing, let her spend a week or two at our shop. I just hope she's up to it. These sideways promotions sometimes keep sliding sideways out the window and leave a bit of damage behind. What I'd... " McLaren was saying as the office door opened to reveal the slim mid-fifties new Superintendent in her brand-new uniform. Before she could say a word, Tony Signorotto stood and spoke.

"Welcome aboard, ma'am. A pleasure to meet you. Senior Sergeant Tony Signorotto, Officer in Charge, Carlton and this is Senior Sergeant Kate McLaren, my second in charge."

Reid thrust out her hand at the same time as speaking. "Thank you, Senior Sergeant, but I'm not in charge of one of Her Majesty's ships. Senior Sergeant McLaren, nice to meet you also," she said quickly shaking hands before moving to the other side of the coffee table and indicating for the two members to sit.

"It's good of you to invite us in to get to know you, ma'am. I'm sure you are looking forward to coming out and looking around the Division. The other stations of... " Signorotto was cut off mid-sentence by the slightly raised hand of the Superintendent who was sitting and looking him directly in the eye.

"This is not the time for social invitations, Senior Sergeant. I believe you have a reputation for getting results on your patch, however, I think that perhaps you should delegate more of your outside policing efforts towards your, let me say, younger and just as competent members like Kate here. After all, she may be a star on the rise, don't you think? Competent and brave if I read your file correctly, Kate, what with that valour award you were presented with."

"Ma'am, I am just a team member at Carlton. I might have been awarded a medal, but if it hadn't been for Senior Sergeant Signorotto guiding and backing me that day, who knows how that situation may have gone down," Kate said with a straight face.

"Don't get me wrong," Reid said looking from one member to the other, "I have been given a total run down on your station and everyone in it by the outgoing Superintendent Phil Stone. I think I am lucky to have such a tight knit unit in my Division. It's just that a situation has arisen where I need Senior Sergeant Signorotto here to oversee, but I want you to run the operation on the ground. It's something that needs a bit of tact along with operational experience. No offence meant here Tony, but we need to keep this person on side, and you do have a bit of a reputation for going in—as they say in America—locked and loaded?"

To Reid's surprise, a big smile lit up Signorotto's face and brought a laugh to Kate McLaren's. "If that means I get results, I have no worries being described as that, Superintendent," a now bemused looking Tony Signorotto replied.

"You've gone in hard and successfully with the Mafia a

while back and with that hijack of the police issue guns, but this time we have a complainant in the form of a High Court judge here in Melbourne. I think running point with Kate will get us further using a bit of subtlety."

"I agree that subtlety probably isn't my best attribute, ma'am, but I back my troops from the office and out on the road," a now slightly peeved Tony Signorotto said in his defence.

"The Government and police hierarchy want everyone in the Department to take a step back and work through things without going in like a bull at a gate. That is where I make the point in the book I wrote," Reid said pointing to *The Modern-Day Police Officer and Community Policing* book on the coffee table. "We need to be able to talk our way through many situations these days, Senior Sergeant, not just go in with a bulldozer. Anyway, the ..."

Tony Signorotto shot back immediately, "With all due respect, ma'am, myself, Kate and members of the Carlton police station live and work in an area where if you don't use the bulldozer as you say now and then, the mafia and every other piece of slime in the inner suburbs will eat you up and spit you out. We are constantly fighting fire with fire every day around Carlton and yes, there are times when your mouth can get you out of trouble but there are even more times when you need to shut a few mouths and that requires force, and the only time you will need that book of yours is to whack some non-believer over the head," Signorotto said raising his voice. Reid sat back with her mouth opening and closing as if she had been slapped in the face.

Kate McLaren looked at her Senior Sergeant and realised that her excitable Italian colleague was about to explode. She jumped into the conversation.

"Ma'am," she said quickly, "What is this story with the High Court judge? Why do you need me involved?" Silence engulfed the office until the heat had dissapated between Signorotto and Reid. The Superintendent dragged her stare from Signorotto and turned her eyes slowly towards Kate.

"Justice Miles Wilson presided over a case last week involving a Romanian drug dealer by the name of Chiril Cel Tradat. He sentenced him to twenty years imprisonment but not before he had been offered a bribe of one hundred thousand dollars to let him go on a technicality. Do either of you know or heard of this Cel Tradat?" Reid asked.

"Chiril the Squirrel," Signorotto said immediately. "Given that name because he runs around everywhere for Bogdan Vulpe, a long-time Romanian crook who hangs around the edges of Carlton but doesn't come in too often because he is no friend of the Italian mafia. Detective Sergeant Max Tyler just gave evidence that helped send him down for the twenty. Good operator, Max. Was a protégé of mine. What's little Chiril's problem?" Signorotto said as he looked with daggers at Reid.

"Well, he is now in the Alfred hospital under police guard with multiple broken bones, a ruptured spleen and kidney as well what looks like permanent brain damage. He is in intensive care," Reid said tersely. "Seeing that you seem to know this character Cel Tradat, perhaps you could enlighten us, Senior Sergeant?"

"Works for Bogdan Vulpe and I would say he has met some new friends that Bogdan sent to make sure he keeps his mouth shut in the can. If you want to know more, ma'am, get Max Tyler in here to explain the intricacies of working with these lowlifes around Carlton and Fitzroy. I'll just toddle back to my desk," Signorotto said with a flourish of his right hand as he stood and walked out of Reid's office briskly and without explanation.

Kate McLaren looked across at her new Superintendent who sat there speechless.

"Ma'am, he really is a top operator. Wears his heart on his sleeve a bit. The only way for you to judge him is to get into a police car with him and do a patrol where he has grown up, married and had kids. The man bleeds for his crew and his suburb."

"A bit more direct than anyone I worked for in the Met, but I am finding out how direct and to the point you Australians are. No one back home would speak to me like he did and to be honest, Kate, no one would be telling me to go and get into a patrol car with him."

"You got it in one, ma'am. This is your home now, not London. You must walk the walk as well as talk the talk. Welcome to Carlton," Kate said smiling at Reid.

Chapter 4

Bogdan Vulpe was sitting in his favourite Romanian restaurant in Melbourne, *Delicios*. If he was honest with himself, which was very hard for a crook like Vulpe to be, it was the only one he knew about.

Vulpe didn't have the plethora of Italian restaurants to choose from like the Sicilian mafia brotherhood that inhabited the suburbs of Carlton and Collingwood. He had to settle for Johnston Street, North Fitzroy in which to hold court. It was late in the afternoon and Vulpe was tucking into a traditional Romanian dish consisting of *Ciorba de burta* followed by *Sarmale*. To any off the street punter this would have meant beef tripe soup and cabbage rolls. It wasn't a surprise to anyone else but a true Romanian that there weren't many Romanian restaurants on the top ten must visit eateries list in Melbourne.

Vulpe hadn't invited anyone else to dine because he had to make an important phone call. He had heard previously that Cel Tradat had been attacked in prison and he wanted details of who did it. He knew it had nothing to do with Elena Rossu. He had ordered his death, not a beating. Stuffing another *sarmale* in his mouth with one hand, he rang through on a burner phone to Rossu.

"What happened to Cel Tradat? Who put him in hospital?"

Rossu was talking quietly from behind a large refrigerator in the prison kitchen. "I only heard that some Romanian inmate was trying to impress you by nearly killing him. That is all I know. Please leave me alone. I just want to live my life in peace."

"This time you didn't have time to do anything, but if he

makes it back to prison, I will expect you to act. Do you understand?" Vulpe said menacingly and then hung up.

Rossu knew she couldn't take any more of these threats. She had to do something about Vulpe and get protection for herself and her daughter. There was no way she could go through with killing anyone. For the time being, the situation had been taken away from her, but she knew the nightmare would return. The only thing she could think of was to go to the Geelong police and ask for help. She would ask to speak to the person in charge and hope he or she could help her.

The next day, Rossu rang through to the prison and told them she had a migraine and would not be in for work. After driving Anna to school, she went immediately to the Corio police station. Parking outside, she calmed herself before entering. She nervously approached the counter and spoke to a young constable behind the plexi-glass partition.

"Excuse me but could I please speak to the person who is in charge here?"

"What is it about? I'll have to let her know before you can see her. She is upstairs and is very busy today," the constable said with an apologetic smile.

"I need to talk to someone because my life is in danger. My daughter's as well," Elena said nervously as she stood shifting from one foot to another.

The constable looked long and hard at Elena then slowly reached for the internal phone.

"Could I get a member from your office to come down to the inquiry counter please? I have a lady here who says her life is being threatened."

"I'll be down in a minute," Detective Sergeant Peter Collins from the Corio CIU said, reaching for his folder.

Within two minutes, the detective was standing in front of the seated Rossu, who he could see was clearly upset.

The detective sat down slowly next to her.

"First off, any person who comes in here and reports a threat against themselves or their family is taken very seriously. Is it a member of your family you wish to report? Maybe your partner or husband?" Collins said thinking along the lines of it being a domestic dispute.

"Can we talk somewhere else rather than out here in the public?" Elena said quietly.

Collins led her into a closed interview room and offered her a seat as he removed a form from his folder which related to domestic violence. Rossu saw the large print on top of the form and reached across the desk and turned it upside down, causing Collins to stop and stare at her.

"This has nothing to do with relatives. The man who is threatening me is a criminal from Melbourne. A Romanian gangster by the name of Bogdan Vulpe."

Collins's memory started to kick in immediately. Vulpe was not a name you could forget easily if you were a detective.

"Why is he threatening you? Vulpe is known very well in criminal circles in Melbourne but not so much down here."

"I am in a situation where he thinks he can blackmail me. I am of Romanian birth, and I am the head chef at Barwon prison. There are certain things he has had me do in passing messages from inmate to inmate. Small things, but now he has contacted me for something much worse. He threatens myself and my daughter and even family back in Romania. That is why I have gone along with him so far, but not anymore. I need help, please."

Between scribbling furiously in his folder with information that Rossu was giving him, he put his head up quickly and asked her the question that was uppermost in his mind.

"What is this thing that is much worse? Passing information from prisoner to prisoner and even to the outside is something that happens all the time down there."

"He contacted me and wanted a prisoner by the name of Chiril Cel Tradat killed. He wanted me to poison his food. I didn't know what to do. I was scared for my family. I was never going to do this but now Cel Tradat is in hospital. He was ... "

"I know all about Cel Tradat," Collins interrupted. "I am the detective investigating the attack. You are going to have to start from the beginning including the phone number he used to ring you on."

"He uses untraceable phones for safety, I think. There was no number," Rossu said with disappointment in her voice.

Fifteen minutes later after Rossu had told Collins the full gist of the demand, he asked her to wait while he made a phone call from another office.

When the phone picked up on the other end, he couldn't keep the delight out of his voice.

"Max Tyler, that you?" Collins said quickly.

"Who's this?" a suspicious Tyler said in reply.

"Mate, Pete Collins. Remember from Detective Training School?"

"Yes, of course. What are you up to? Hear you are down Geelong way. What can I do for you?"

"I heard you put one of Bogdan Vulpes's boys away for twenty years. Well done."

"You didn't ring me up to say well done. Come on, with that happy tone in your voice I think there may be something else, eh?" Tyler said.

"I think I have someone down here at Corio that you will want to talk to. Someone that may help you a lot regarding Vulpe himself."

"Tell me more my friend, tell me more," Max Tyler said reaching out to his desk to grab a pen and paper. "If I have to come down the highway, I might even shout you lunch."

"Once you talk to this informant, only the biggest and juiciest steak at the Elephant and Castle will suffice," a laughing Collins said.

"You're on, mate."

Chapter 5

Superintendent Anne Reid walked through the door of the Carlton police station unannounced to anybody. With her was her Staff Officer, Inspector Vince Anderson who was newly promoted from the Major Crime Squad. They were both in plain clothes. Reid stood in the very modern and clean foyer as Anderson waited behind two civilians who were in the middle of having some forms signed by Senior Constable Chloe Schaeffer at the inquiry counter.

"Won't be a minute, sir," the Chloe said with an efficient tone, looking up at Anderson.

"That's fine. Not an inquiry. When you've finished, can you let Senior Sergeant Signorotto know that Superintendent Reid is here to see him," Anderson said, indicating behind him.

So, this is the new braid, is it? Schaeffer thought as she nodded back to the Inspector before turning her face towards Reid.

"Do it now, but as the bosses here are very security conscious, could I have some identification from both of you please. With all due respect, I have never had the pleasure of meeting either of you before. Both the Senior Sergeants would rip strips off me if I let you any further into the building without checking your *bona fides*," she said smiling.

Both Anderson and Reid produced their police identifications. As Schaeffer looked at both, Reid spoke to her.

"Quite right too, Senior. Would have been disappointed if you hadn't asked for identification," she said.

"Can't be too careful, ma'am," the Senior Constable said

as the civilian thanked her and departed through the front door with a signed Statutory Declaration. "Best of luck with that, Bert. Hope it does the trick." Schaeffer picked up the phone, rang through to the upstairs office area and seconds later put the phone down and spoke.

"Boss will be down in a second, ma'am."

"Thank you, Senior. By the way, what was that civilian needing a Statutory Declaration for?" Reid said.

"Just trying to appeal a parking ticket he got from the council. The person who put the ticket on his car didn't see the disabled sticker hanging from his rear-view mirror. He was taking his wife shopping."

"Why would the police get involved? That's a problem between the council and him, not us," Reid replied with an inquisitive look on her face.

Chloe Schaeffer looked from the Superintendent to the Inspector with a smile on her face.

"Bert's a pensioner. He just scrapes by, and he was just doing a bit of shopping for himself and his wife, who by the way can't leave the house because she has rapid onset MS. If he just sent a letter to the council, they'd probably ignore him, so I worded the Statutory Declaration for him, signed it and added a line or two about his situation. There's a lot of people around here that need looking after, ma'am. Senior Sergeant Signorotto expects us to not only catch crooks but also to look after our own. As the bosses here say, it's not about just solving crime—it's about solving problems."

Tight knit station and community, Reid thought just as Tony Signorotto appeared in the foyer.

"Welcome to Carlton, ma'am. You too, Inspector...?" Signorotto said, giving the Superintendent's staff officer a chance to introduce himself.

"Vince Anderson, Tony. Superintendent Reid's new Staff Officer," he said shaking hands.

"Ex Major Crime, aren't you?" Signorotto said with a quizzical look on his face.

"Yeah, I am, Tony. Have I bumped into you before?"

"No, but I make it my business to know every crook in town and every up and comer from the ranks, Vince. Good to meet you."

"Senior Sergeant didn't mean to spring a surprise visit on you, but we need to have a meeting about that judge I was telling you about. Things have come to light. I've got Kate McLaren coming in on her rest day and I've got Max Tyler dropping in, also. You apparently know this Bogdan Vulpe on the street level and Inspector Anderson knows him from his time at Major Crime. How about we all sit down and have a round table conference somewhere," Reid said just as Max Tyler came through the front door and Kate McLaren appeared through the back door dressed in a windcheater and jeans.

"Well, if the gang's all here, let's head upstairs to the conference room," Signorotto said as he motioned with his hand towards the stairs at the back of the foyer.

As they all started to walk, Reid turned and spoke to another member standing beside Schaeffer. "If you could come upstairs and make some tea and coffee for us all, please."

The older female Police Reservist looked up at the Superintendent. "There's plenty of tea and coffee in the conference room and I'm sure you are all quite capable of making your own while we deal with the taxpayers down here," Reservist Jill Norton said with a straight face.

Reid turned to Kate McLaren and was about to say something regarding Jill Norton, but Kate beat her to it.

"Tell you all about our Jill later but suffice to say she is the other female Valour Award recipient here at Carlton. Without her, this place would descend into chaos."

"You don't ask favours here, do you?" Reid said, shaking her head.

Chapter 6

The phone call came through to Bogdan Vulpe as he was driving his imported Romanian Dacia Duster SUV to his Fitzroy North home. Vulpe was a loyal Romanian and although it had cost him a lot of money to import the Dacia and then have it converted to right hand drive, he didn't care. It wasn't the greatest car that had been built in Europe, but it was built in Romania and that was all that mattered. It drove like a truck and handled like a pig, but in his mind, it was far better than anything the Russians could put out or even the Czech Republic with their Skoda brand.

"Cel Tradat is brain dead," Anton Funan said over the phone as Vulpe listened on his car speaker.

"What are his chances of speaking sense again?" Vulpe asked cautiously.

"According to a nurse contact of mine at the Alfred, he'll be drooling for the rest of his life."

"That's one less problem then. Get onto our solicitors and make sure that whoever beat his brains in gets an all-expenses defence when he comes up on charges. Not that I give a fuck about the outcome, but we must make it look that if one of our brothers gets charged with anything down there then we'll look after him. Understand?"

"Understood, boss. Who do you want to take his place as the export man now that we can get back to business?" Funan said, thinking that Vulpe must have someone in mind.

"For the time being, you and Dalca will be doing two jobs."

"What's the second job, boss?" a now confused Funan replied.

"We have Romanian pride on the line here, Anton. You and Dalca didn't convince that judge to go along with your money offer so now you will have to fix that also," Vulpe said as he switched the car speaker back to the phone while he got out of his SUV in the garage at his home, smiling as he smelt what his wife Irina was cooking for dinner. The aroma of stewed trout cooked in tomato sauce was wafting out of the kitchen window. A smile lit up his face as he walked through the front door.

"We have business to finish with that judge. When I am through with him, he will never sit in a court again. By ignoring you, he ignored me. I had already told some of my wealthier Romanian brothers that Cel Tradat would be getting off the charge or it would be changed to another much lesser one. I won't have him ignoring me. This judge must pay a price for going against me. Something needs to be done to show we are the big player in town."

"What do you mean? I thought with a brain dead Cel we could forget the judge."

Vulpe's smile disappeared altogether as he continued to speak. "You get yourself and Dalca to the office tonight at nine sharp. We need to resolve this matter," Vulpe said as he stared at the bottom of a glass of Romanian Burebista Negra shiraz that he had just drained in two mouthfuls.

"Boss, this is crazy. What was the point of offering a judge money in the first place? He has been on the bench for years getting paid much more than that. Both Dalca and I checked him out through the public records office. Last year he was paid three times that for two months overseeing some Royal Commission into the building industry. Money won't work with this guy. Just let it go. He's what they call in the legal circles a straight shooter. He's too upstanding to even consider it. I knew at the time we had no chance. You've got to understand that this isn't Romania where you just go around threatening and kidnapping these guys and their families. It brings too much heat on us," a despairing Anton Funan said.

"You just said the magic word, Anton. The word family. He will learn that he shouldn't take the safety of his family for granted. He might not have taken any notice of the one hundred thousand dollars, but I have no doubt he will pay ten times that much when it comes to his family and their future. Get to the office tonight," Vulpe said just before disconnecting the call.

Anton Funan sat back in his car with a sigh of despair. He had no choice but to contact Codrin Dalca and do as Vulpe asked. He would try once more to talk him out of any revenge plans so they could just concentrate on what they did best, and that was making huge amounts of money with the importation and distribution of drugs and firearms through the cleaning business. With their network, no one was going to interfere with the importation of cleaning goods that were labelled for the Cleanstyle Industrial Cleaning Company. The government contracts both state and federal had been signed and delivered via large cash payments to politicians in both Melbourne and Canberra. The fact that many shipments were tagged for the business did not mean they all contained cleaning chemicals. There was an ever-increasing market for drugs, firearms and many other illegal imports in Australia and Vulpe's organisation was only supplying the goods that were wanted. Cel Tradat had made a stupid mistake by being caught with drug precursor chemicals at his own house and had paid the price by being charged with possession of amounts which led to the sentence he received. Some of the imports through the docks would now be re-directed through other businesses, but in smaller amounts for the next six months or so.

Funan picked up his phone and rang through to Dalca.

"The boss wants us at his office tonight at nine. Wants to talk revenge about this fucking judge that put Cel Tradat away. Why I don't know. Just wish he'd forget it," Funan said angrily.

"The boss is the boss. Might be crazy, but I'm not telling him that. See you there at nine," Dalca said.

Nothing good's going to come out of this, Funan thought.

Chapter 7

Superintendent Reid led the meeting from the onset. It was obvious to all around the table when she began that she had the background for dealing with this type of scenario.

"I'll start by saying this. We have a situation where a Supreme Court judge, His Honour Justice Miles Wilson has, along with his wife, been threatened and intimidated in the car park of Donovans restaurant in St. Kilda ten days ago. The threat, although given subtly by one of the males involved was partly captured on the restaurant's CCTV and shows quite clearly that it was directed at Wilson in relation to the case he subsequently handed his decision down on days later in connection to the now hospitalised and permanently brain damaged criminal Chiril Cel Tradat. I have gathered you all together to discuss operational plans because there is a link between the threat and a situation at Barwon State prison. I'll let Detective Sergeant Max Tyler take up on the connection, but before I do, I can see a questioning look on the face of Senior Sergeant Signorotto and I think I can answer his question without him even asking it. The reason we are here at the Carlton police station is because Judge Wilson is a resident of Carlton and is going to need that connection with the station which is what I was talking about the other day before you removed yourself from my office, Senior Sergeant," Reid said looking directly at the slightly reddening Tony Signorotto. After some sideways glances around the table, Max Tyler began to speak.

"At Melbourne CIU, I have been working directly with the Major Crime Squad and, until his recent promotion to Inspector, Vince Anderson here," indicating the suited member sitting next to the Superintendent. With a lot of help and cooperation between the CIU and the MCS we not only got in behind the scenes of a well-known Melbourne crime boss, Bogdan Vulpe, we made a significant arrest when we raided Cel Tradat's house. He would never admit where the drug ingredients came from but with charging him with large scale possession, it meant he ended up in a higher court and subsequently got himself twenty years behind bars. Unfortunately for him it was just the beginning of his troubles."

"Where does Vulpe come into this beside the fact that Cel Tradat worked for him?" Kate McLaren chipped in.

"Getting to that, Kate. I've been down to Corio CIU to see the detective who is the lead investigator on Cel Tradat's assault. They are about to charge an inmate down there who stars on CCTV giving Chiril a belting with bag full of gym weights. Turns out he's a young Romanian who thought he would impress Vulpe with maybe getting into his good books one day. If the assault had taken place in that spot days before he would have got away with it, but the prison has installed some of those small quick-fix Wi Fi cameras which they put up in no time. No hard wiring so no workmen. This idiot never realised that he was doing the bashing live on camera. The guards raced down there but the damage had already been done. Turns out that Vulpe had never asked him to do it, but here's the really interesting part. Apparently Vulpe had been in contact with the female cook who runs the prison kitchen and who has relatives here and in Romania. He was blackmailing her for some bits and pieces of prison information but suddenly when Cel Tradat hits the place he wants him knocked. He told her that he wanted Cel Tradat killed with poison or something. She was never going to do it and then the bashing took place and Cel Tradat was taken away.

"With me so far?" Tyler said looking around the room at the slow nods he was getting back from Signorotto and McLaren.

"To join up the dots in the story, this cook by the name of Elena Rossu, ends up talking to the Corio CIU and makes a statement putting Vulpe in for the threat to kill."

"Dangerous thing to do. Gutsy but dangerous," Tony Signorotto said suddenly.

"Agree Tony but the MCS together with Witness Security have taken her and her daughter under their wing. Relocated them already. What we are going to do next is arrest Vulpe for the threat to incite the murder of Cel Tradat and grab both of his offsiders for the bribe proposal on Wilson. I know he's in hospital and will never give evidence, but this Elena Russo will. She just wants a free life in Australia and is prepared to go on the stand."

"People," Superintendent Reid said, interrupting Max Tyler. "What you will have probably realised is that we have the threat to kill with Vulpe and the bribe threat with his two lieutenants who were recognised on CCTV in St. Kilda. We have a good chance of a conviction on Vulpe because he doesn't know at this stage that Rossu has given him up and we have two of his boys, namely Codrin Dalca and Anton Funan at the restaurant. Wilson has also seen Funan sitting in on the court case and recognised him as one of the two that approached him in St. Kilda. What I want to do is get the three of them off the street as quick as possible. They can all sit in prison until whenever their court cases come up."

"Ma'am," I totally get where you are headed with this, but I don't think they will be sitting in the can till their cases come up. The courts are log jammed with cases. In England it might be different, but here I'll bet you, excuse the pun, London to a brick that the three of them make bail very quickly. This state government is toothless as far as keeping these types off the street. Myself and my team here are up against it all the time. It's like a revolving door. Put them in one side and they are back past you onto the footpath so fast it makes your head spin. What's your opinion, Inspector Anderson? You've dealt with heavies in the MCS. What do you envisage happening to them when they come up for a bail hearing?" Signorotto said deferring to the Superintendent's staff officer.

"You don't think we can get a conviction?" Reid said with a worried look on her face.

"Oh, I think they will be convicted, but if their trials don't come up for months or even a year, no magistrate in Victoria will let them languish behind bars on those charges. Vulpe will deny contacting Russo and we all know he didn't order Cel Tradat bashed and now with him hospitalised, it depends on one very scared cook. No doubt we can get a conviction on the other two for bribery, but again, I can't see them behind bars on a case where no one was hurt. Terrified yes, but not hurt, Signorotto said."

"Working on crooks like these ma'am, we need something a lot more intimidating and dangerous before the lower courts will do anything. I'd have to agree with Tony here. They will all make bail even with the Department screaming blue murder," Anderson replied.

After a short period of silence, Reid spoke. "Okay, but we must show all of them they can't go around doing this. Arrest them, lock them up and we'll hope the courts see it our way and don't post bail. While this is going on, I want you, Kate, to pay a visit to Judge Wilson and work up a liaison with him. If the bribe case doesn't come up for a year, then I'm sure you and he will be great friends by then."

"Not a problem, ma'am. Get on it straight away," Kate McLaren said.

Vince Anderson spoke up. "We are going to have to work quick here, people. I had already arranged phone taps on Dalca and Funan and we hit pay dirt yesterday. Vulpe wants both at the office tonight to plan revenge on Wilson and Funan. He's on tape talking to Dalca arranging it. The office will mean the Cleanstyle office at 342 Nicholson Street. They are getting there at nine tonight. I have the SOG as backup, but I think it would be good if Max can make the bust on Vulpe and Tony, if you can get a few members in, we'll take down the other two at the same time. I think seeing Max again after Cel Tradat's sentence will show Vulpe that we are following him closer than his shadow. We need to all be back here at seven tooled up and ready. What do you think, ma'am?" Anderson said looking at his Superintendent.

"Sounds like a plan, Inspector. Just one thing though. Where I come from the Superintendent leads from the front. I will be there side by side with Senior Sergeant Signorotto. Don't worry Tony, I just wanted to put into place something your fellow Senior Sergeant suggested."

"What's that, Superintendent?" Signorotto shot back with.

"Apparently I have to walk the walk with you, not just talk the talk," Reid said with a smile at Signorotto's puzzled face.

"Not a problem, ma'am, but are you qualified with the Department here regarding carrying a nine-millimetre firearm?" Signorotto asked with half a smile on his face. A lot of other officers would have backed off when they were told about the lengthy court delay.

"Not with the Smith and Wesson that is used here, but I am with a Glock and with the shotgun that I carried back in the Met. Think I'll bring both tonight," Reid said.

Chapter 8

Max Tyler took Vince Anderson aside in the backyard of the Carlton police station as the various members came out to the cars prior to the raid to arrest Vulpe and his offsiders. Parked ominously near the gate were two black Toyota Land Cruisers belonging to the SOG.

Seven of the black clad members stood by their vehicles in an almost military fashion clutching their Remington pump action shotguns. The senior member was walking towards Tyler and Anderson to partake in the briefing that was about to be given by Superintendent Reid. They knew they were only back-up but as one of them had said earlier, *if you go into the forest be prepared to hunt bear, not rabbits!*

"Sir, how do you want to play this. A quick knock on the door and a shout to those inside to come out then hit it with the sledgehammer if they don't comply after twenty seconds or so?"

"If you like, Max but from my experience I'll probably have a sudden attack of laryngitis just before we go through the front door. Happens every time and I don't know why," the experienced ex Major Crime Squad member said with a grin on his face. "Never give a sucker an even break, Max. I don't trust my grandmother sometimes, let alone snakes like we'll find in this place. Also, there won't be any back door entrance. We'll cover it but, but mate, we never use the Tradesman's entrance. We are the professionals, so we always go through the front door."

Just after eight forty-five p.m. the SOG radioed that they were in position in the alleyway behind the Cleanstyle factory at 342 Nicholson Street, Fitzroy. They knew that they would only be called upon if it turned into a firefight, but they were happy just to be on the road and not in the office. As they settled back into the darkness, four unmarked police SUVs pulled up in Nicholson Street a few doors down from Cleanstyle.

Vince Anderson stepped out carrying the sledgehammer, or as the experienced members called them, *the front door key.* Followed by each crew, he went to the wooden door, coughed twice and then swung the sledgehammer to a spot directly opposite the lock. The door splintered immediately and swung open. Anderson stood back and let the others in.

The fully kitted crew split into their teams. First was Max Tyler and Chloe Schaeffer, then, after dropping the sledgehammer, Vince Anderson stepped to one side along with Tony Signorotto. All members including four back up officers, who were standing against the wall, immediately drew their firearms and aimed them towards the conference room in front of them where they could hear the sounds of chairs being knocked over.

Holding a Smith and Wesson Police and Military nine-millimetre pistol in her right hand, Superintendent Anne Reid lifted a megaphone she held in her left hand and spoke directly at the door in front of them.

"Police. Every person will come out of the room one at a time with their hands raised. We are armed and will not hesitate to shoot if you come out carrying weapons. Come out now," she said tersely.

The door slowly opened, and a pistol was thrown onto the floor at her feet as Codrin Dalca came out with his hands raised. He was followed by Anton Funan who also threw a firearm on the ground. Neither man made a move except for the shaking of their bodies as they saw the armed members in front of them. Reid lowered the megaphone as Signorotto, gun still raised, spoke.

"Where's Vulpe?" he said as the ominous sound of a door closing at the rear of the premises could be heard.

Funan, who was behind Dalca stood with his hands raised but with his head indicated to the back where the sound came from.

"Down on the floor and put your hands out to your side. Now," Anderson barked.

Both hoons did so very quickly and were handcuffed immediately.

"Looks like Vulpe got away," Reid said quietly with a disappointed sound in her voice.

"Come with me, ma'am," Signorotto said as he walked out the front door followed by the puzzled Superintendent, along with Max Tyler. They walked quickly around to the rear of the premises where they could hear a male swearing at the top of his voice. Lying on the ground, face down in the dirt was the spreadeagled form of Bogdan Vulpe. Standing with a black boot between Vulpe's shoulder blades was the towering form of the SOG Sergeant who was holding his shotgun next to Vulpe's right ear. Max Tyler stepped up to the crook, took out his handcuffs, attached them tightly to his prisoner and then rolled him uncomfortably onto his back.

"Remember me, Bogdan?" Tyler said as Vulpe's eyes widened.

"You fucking piece of shit. What's this about? I was just coming out here for some fresh air and this big prick here sticks a shotty in my face," Vulpe said loudly as he looked up at the SOG member.

"No weapon ma'am," the SOG sergeant said shaking his head. Vulpe continued to scream.

"I'm on my own property you fucking scum. I'll sue you all for this. You too bitch," he said as he spat on the ground next to Reid's shoe. The Superintendent stepped forward, wiped the sole of her shoe in the spittle and then proceeded to wipe the shoe on Vulpe's shirt. She then spoke to Tyler who looked at her in disbelief because of the shoe act.

"He's all yours, Detective Sergeant. Tell him in one syllable words what's happening. Nice and slow so he understands. All he seems to know are swear words." Reid and Signorotto stepped back as Vulpe was lifted to his feet.

"Bogdan Vulpe, you are under arrest for making threats to kill against Chiril Cel Tradat. You don't have to say anything, but what you do say will be taken down and may be given in evidence. Do you understand this?"

An evil smile came across Vulpe's face as he spoke. "Oh, I understand all right. So will you, bitch!" *You've just changed my revenge plans.*

Chapter 9

The interview with Bogdan Vulpe was going the way Max Tyler thought it would. It was like getting blood out of a stone. Strictly name, rank and serial number.

"Okay, Bogdan, I have previously asked you if you want a solicitor present, but you haven't answered me. I'll ask you one more time and if you don't answer I will keep going with the interview."

"I don't want a solicitor, because I haven't done anything. You're the person who will want one for arresting me on my own premises for no reason."

"You have been arrested for making threats to kill Chiril Cel Tradat who is an inmate at Barwon State Prison. Have you got anything you want to say in relation to this?"

"An inmate of the Alfred hospital would be more like it. What's it got to do with me?"

"We have a witness who will give evidence that you have been blackmailing them and that you ordered Cel Tradat to be poisoned in prison," Tyler said realising that he really had no choice but to drag Elena Rossus' name into the interview.

A smile broke out on Vulpe's face before he spoke next. "So, you're going to charge me on the evidence of some low life female cook from prison. You've got to be kidding me. My solicitor will tear her to shreds in the witness box."

"Just so you know Vulpe, she no longer works there. She is now in protective custody where neither you nor any of your offsiders will get to her."

"She'll never give evidence against me. Too many relatives. She wouldn't dare."

"I remind you Vulpe that you are being recorded here. Sounds very much like another threat. Be careful."

"I am of Romanian birth, Tyler. Don't think that you can scare me. Neither you nor those two bitches can."

Tyler thought for a moment before he replied.

"Who are you referring to when you say those two bitches?"

"No bitch wipes their shoes on me and gets away with it. Now either charge me or let me go. You didn't get me with a weapon, so you've got no case for keeping me locked up. Maybe for a couple of days, but I'll get bail, no sweat."

Max Tyler turned off the recording machine as two burly uniforms lifted the still handcuffed Vulpe kicking and screaming onto his feet and back to his cell at the Carlton police station. He headed back through the Watch House where he bumped into Tony Signorotto.

"Tony, can we have a chat. We might have a bit of a problem with Vulpe I reckon."

"Yeah, sure. Come on upstairs. I've just finished charging Dalca and Funan with the threats to Wilson. Funan especially didn't mind saying how stupid he thought Vulpe was in threatening a Supreme Court judge."

As they walked up the stairs to the conference room, Tyler continued.

"I think that mad Romanian is more upset with our new Superintendent than he is with Cel Tradat or Wilson."

"What do you mean? Just because she ran the raid? We were all there. He should be pissed off, but with all of us. Why her?"

"She wiped her shoe on him after he spat on her. I could tell by looking at him, Tony. His eyes just rolled back in his head over it. Must be a macho Romanian thing or something. We're going to have to really fight bail on him. Going to be hard with only one witness, no gun and on his own property. I know he's got a long rap sheet, but still, I think we can put the other two away until they come up for trial, but I'm not so sure about Vulpe," a worried sounding Tyler said as they approached Reid, Anderson and McLaren who were seated at the table.

Superintendent Reid turned to the group and, after picking up a copy of the proposed charge sheets on the three, spoke to them all.

"That was well done tonight by everyone. I was impressed. What's the next step now, Inspector Anderson?" she said deferring to the former Major Crime Squad member.

"Well, Vulpe will be coming up to the Magistrates Court the day after tomorrow on charges of threats to kill via a telephone communication service. He unfortunately didn't have a weapon on him, and it looks as though he used a burner phone to talk to Russo. We did find a Romanian Carpati pistol in his office, but again, no prints and it was in an open locker where anybody could have put it. It will all depend on who does the hearing. The other two will be a no brainer because they threatened the judge. Two witnesses there and they were both seen throwing out their pistols when we arrested them so even with good rep from some bent solicitor, I think they'll stay put. We won't put them up with Vulpe. Tony and I have noticed something about Funan. We reckon we could turn him because he's had enough of Vulpe not taking advice. We'll keep him on the backburner."

"Okay. I think we will call it a night then," Reid said.

"Just need to talk to you, ma'am, about that shoe wiping episode. Need to give you a heads up," a concerned Tyler said to Reid as he started to relate what had happened in the interview room to the whole crew. "It's about Romanian macho ego."

Tony Signorotto listened intently with a very concerned look on his face.

Chapter 10

"His heart didn't really seem in the threat, I must say," His Honour Justice Miles Wilson said to Kate McLaren as he sat himself down on the Chesterfield winged armchair in his study, at the same time as inviting her to sit on one opposite. "Tea or coffee, Senior Sergeant?"

"Coffee would be most appreciated," Kate replied as she felt herself sink into the expensive dark brown leather chair. Looking around the study reminded her of being inside the State Library. Every wall was covered by floor to ceiling mahogany bookcases which were to the point of overflowing. Built into the bottom of one bookcase was a beautiful desk with a gold filigree writing area. On top of one part of the desk was a thirty-inch Apple computer which was displaying what looked like a legal document of some sort.

"The fact is that one stood on the other side of my car frightening my wife Helen to pieces, and I won't have that. Speaking of the lady herself, here she is with some coffee," he said as Helen Wilson walked into the room with a large plunger of coffee which was giving off a beautiful aroma. As she placed the tray down, she walked over to Kate and shook hands with her.

"That smells good," Kate said as Helen Wilson handed her a cup. "A lot better than what we have at the station, I bet."

"My brother is a Senior Sergeant down at Williamstown," Helen Wilson said with a smile. "So I know all about poor coffee because he tells me every time he comes here for tea."

"Law runs in the family then?" Kate said inquiringly.

"Oh, yes," Judge Wilson replied. "I get it in the neck from

him all the time. He says he arrests them, and I let them go."

"Well, I'm here to talk about the one you gave twenty years to, Your Honour," Kate replied.

"Please, Kate. Now that we have met each other at the door it's Miles and Helen, I insist. Not in court now. To be honest, for the amount of drug paraphernalia that Cel Tradat had at his home, you didn't have to be a Rhodes scholar to know what he and his cronies were up to. Lucky I only gave him twenty. You people go to such lengths to catch these people, I can't understand why some of my legal brothers and sisters don't do what I do and throw the key away on them."

"You probably don't know what has happened to him since sentencing though do you?" Kate said.

"No, I don't, Kate. Please tell me," a surprised Miles Wilson said.

Kate McLaren explained in detail what had happened to Cel Tradat and the involvement of Bogdan Vulpe since the court case. She also showed the judge and his wife pictures of the three. All of the pictures had them displaying their police photo numbers, front on and from either side.

"I remember that character Vulpe staring down from the gallery like some sort of demented idiot. The one who leant on the roof of my car on Helen's side outside the restaurant was also in the gallery. Threatening me is one thing but doing it in front of my wife was something else. If I hadn't been going to the farewell retirement function for a fellow judge and wasn't dressed in a dinner suit, I would have got out of my car and given one of them a decent belting. I do hold a third-degree black belt in Kung Fu. If only there had been an alleyway or such, I would... "

"That's enough, Miles. You are kidding yourself when you

talk about taking them on. I would have spent the next hour with the first aid kit from the back of the Bentley just wrapping you up," Helen Wilson said as Kate burst into laughter.

"What I am really here about," Kate said, "is that although Vulpe and his offsiders have been arrested, charged and are in custody regarding the threat to you two and the phone threat to Cel Tradat, we aren't prepared to take any chances. No offence to you or your fellow judges, Miles, we in the Force don't have the same confidence regarding some of the Magistrates that might hear bail applications for these people. We are not at all confident of Vulpe staying behind bars till his trial comes up. One of the other two, Anton Funan is the one that you say didn't sound too convincing and we may have plans for him regarding turning State's evidence. We know Vulpe's track record with the lower courts and greasing official palms and he is the bigger of the fish by a long way. I hope I haven't shocked you with this?"

"Not at all, Kate. I'll make some very discreet inquiries through a third party. One of my staff will be back in touch. No promises though."

"Thank you, Miles, but in the meantime, my offsider, Senior Sergeant Tony Signorotto wants to get some of our techs in here to set up an emergency video link. If you think there is anyone suspicious nosing around or coming to your door, you will only have to press the button or whatever and it will light up the switchboard at Carlton like a Christmas tree. You live in Carlton and Tony and I take the safety of our residents very, very seriously. This all okay with you?"

"Probably not so much for me, Kate, but I do appreciate it for Helen here. I've got no fear of these lowlifes and they should realise that I will only take it out on their fellow crims with longer sentences if they threaten my family."

"Thanks once again, Miles, if you could make that phone call today it would be good. Vulpe is up for bail tomorrow morning at the Melbourne Magistrates court. We can only put up the best scenario regarding bail, which we will be doing vigorously," Kate said before standing and saying goodbye.

Chapter 11

Tony Signorotto, Max Tyler and Kate McLaren walked up the steps to the Melbourne Magistrates Court shortly after nine a.m. the next morning. They were going straight to the Prosecutor's office to reinforce what the informant, Max Tyler and the Prosecutor, Sergeant Don Jones would say to rebut any attempt by Vulpe to gain bail. As they got to the top step, Kate's phone rang. Looking at it she recognized the number of Judge Miles Wilson.

"Kate, sorry about not getting back to you but it took me forever to find out who is doing Vulpe's bail hearing. Turns out it is a relatively new one by the name of Alexa Mitrea. She was a part time barrister with the present State Government until she got promoted very quickly to the bench of the Lower Court after being recommended by a member of Parliament who has since been stood down for corruption."

"That's an interesting piece of information. I know the M.P you are talking about without going into names over the phone. He had connections to several international mafia figures here and overseas so it's probably on the cards that Vulpe would have his details in his phone."

"I decided to do a bit of Googling on her, and it turns out that she is of Romanian heritage and has folks living back in Bucharest. Normally I would pass right over that, but it raised alarm bells with me. You can obviously guess why. She didn't return any of my calls even after I basically told her clerk it was important. Just a heads up for you, Kate. I can't be seen to be involved any more but I just wanted to let you know."

"I'll let you know how we get on," Kate said as she ended

the call and turned to the others. "There could be something going on behind the scenes with this Tony. Vulpe is a big dealer in the drugs scene here, but it sounds to me like he's working the legal side of it to. A new Magistrate with Romanian heritage is doing the hearing. I don't like this," she said to the others.

"How do you know about the Magistrate?" the Prosecutor said.

"A good contact just told me. Said to be aware."

After fifteen minutes of talking behind closed doors, they emerged and walked into the bail hearing court. Already in the courtroom were Vulpe, handcuffed and seated next to his barrister. He looked across at the Prosecution team and spoke.

"These cuffs will be off soon. Then we'll see who's who in this town, you losers."

Tony Signorotto began to stand and say something in reply, but a hand on his arm from the Prosecutor pulled him back into his chair. As he sat down, the Magistrate's door opened, and Alexa Mitrea walked in quickly and sat at the Bench. Without looking at Vulpe, she turned her eyes towards the Prosecution.

"Let's get on with this," she said very quickly in a nervous sounding voice.

Kate McLaren looked across at a beaming Bogdan Vulpe and got the distinct smell of corruption wafting across the courtroom.

Vulpe's barrister spoke for ten minutes in his application for bail stating that his client was willing to put up a substantial surety to gain his freedom. Together with the facts that he was on his own property and there was no direct link to any firearm, he concluded that the bench had no option but to grant bail.

"Your reply, Mr Prosecutor? I think you will have to put up a very good case to rebut Mr. Vulpe's one," the Magistrate said without looking up at anyone as she tapped on her notebook computer.

"Your Worship, I reject your implication. It sounds as if you have made up your mind without even hearing our application!" the Prosecutor said angrily.

Mitrea waved her hand absentmindedly towards him as she kept typing.

"Ma'am, Bogdan Vulpe has made threats to a prisoner at Barwon State prison through a third party whom we have had to put into witness protection and we..."

"What about the facts that he was on his own property, and I believe was not the only person who had access to the firearm the police located?" Mitrea said sharply.

"Ma'am, yes, they are relevant points but... " the Prosecutor pointed out before being cut off mid-sentence for the second time.

"Extremely relevant I should have thought, Mr. Prosecutor. All you have in an attempt to deny bail is this third-party witness who you say is under witness protection. I think really, the only item on the agenda in relation to this is what bail is set at, don't you?" Mitrea said looking up with a slight smile on her face.

"Ma'am, could I have a minute please to talk to the police involved?"

"Yes, but hurry it up. There are a lot more cases on the list today."

The Prosecutor turned quickly to Signorotto, McLaren and Tyler.

"She never had any intention of denying bail. Vulpe is almost laughing at us. How did she know about the firearm in his office if someone hasn't been speaking to her privately? The only thing we can do now is go for a large surety on him," he said turning back to face the bench.

"Ma'am, we would ask for his passport to be surrendered and a surety of no less than $250,000."

Mitrea looked at Vulpe who's face now bore a scowl obviously about his passport being put on the line. Seconds later she turned back to the prosecution table.

"Charges aren't serious enough for a surrender of his passport. Mr. Vulpe has relatives in Romania and may wish to visit his parents there before his trial comes up. I'll set bail at five thousand dollars, Mr. Prosecutor. Take those handcuffs off the applicant immediately. Next application please, Clerk," she said quickly to the Clerk of Courts sitting down below her. Vulpe suddenly spoke out loud to the prosecution table.

"Five thousand? Paid more than that for a night out with friends at a restaurant."

Tony Signorotto, by this stage, was past being held back by the Prosecutor. He turned and took several steps towards Vulpe and his barrister, who, upon seeing the burly figure approach, tried to step away but at the same time spilled all his papers on the court floor.

"Didn't know dogs were so expensive to take out, Vulpe. But then again, they would eat garbage," Signorotto said before turning and walking away from the now enraged Romanian towards the exit along with his team.

"Senior Sergeant, release this man from handcuffs now," Mitrea called out loudly from the bench.

"I'll find some keys immediately, ma'am. Just have to take this call from Judge Wilson first."

The look on the Mitrea's face was one of shock. She made no reply though as the Prosecution team departed the court to the sounds of Vulpe swearing and kicking over furniture.

"She's in his pocket all right," Kate McLaren said. "First the reference to the firearm and then talking about Vulpe's relatives in Romania. How does she know if his parents are alive or not? Miles Wilson is going to love this bit of information," she said as she pressed his phone number in her mobile phone.

"Time for a coffee, people," Signorotto said with a smile on his face "First things first. Need a caffeine kick before I even think about looking for handcuff keys."

Chapter 12

"If we want to be sure about Vulpe ending up in gaol, I think we are going to have to either get him on fresh charges or collect a lot more information on his set up," Vince Anderson said from his side of the crowded conference table, situated in the office of the Deputy Commissioner for Crime, high up in Police Headquarters.

Around him sat a mini task force that had been put together on instructions from the Chief Commissioner's office. Beside Anderson, there were all the people that had partaken in the arrests of Vulpe, Dalca and Funan. It consisted of Max Tyler, Kate McLaren, Tony Signorotto and Chloe Schaffer. Heading the group was Superintendent Anne Reid, who spoke as soon as Anderson had finished.

"I think I may have mortally offended Vulpe by wiping my shoe on him after he spat at me, but if that helps unbalance him, all the better. Does anyone here know how we can get rid of this piece of vermin from the streets on a permanent basis. It's too risky trying to infiltrate anyone into his cleaning company because as far as his employment records go, he only employs anyone with a Romanian background. He's not doing this to be nice though. From what Max Tyler has told us after arresting Dalca and Funan, I think he likes to employ people who he can hold something over. Would that be right, Detective Sergeant?" Reid asked.

"After his arrest, the Feds went right through his businesses with a fine-tooth comb. What they did find were the lists of his employees, all of whom have relatives living back in the home country. It's amazing that most of them don't quit, seeing that he pays them a pittance. They did interview a couple of women that do some office cleaning at some of the contracts. They'd worked for him for a number of years and every time they tried to leave his employ, family members for both of them were threatened both here and back home. I think though, Senior Sergeant Signorotto may have an idea that we can use. It will sound a bit strange after we went to a lot of work to nab them all, but I can see it helping us. Tony?" All members including the Deputy Commissioner focused on the serious looking Senior Sergeant.

"Simple. We let both Dalca and Funan apply for bail and we either don't appeal it or we put up very little resistance."

Some members looked at Tony and were gobsmacked. One who was beginning to think that Signorotto thought outside the square was his new boss, Anne Reid.

"You keep sailing against the wind, Senior Sergeant," Reid said. I've only known you for a short time but please, tell us your idea."

"Vulpe likes his regulars around him, ma'am. Let's give them back to him. From the interview I did with Funan, he's had enough of the stupid ideas Vulpe keeps coming up with. During it, I got a real sense that if we helped him, he would help us. The only way to do this is to get him to apply for bail again, albeit with our encouragement and get him out from under the Romanian. He knows he's facing serious gaol time and I reckon if I meet with him again, I could turn him. He's got a long wait in the Remand Section before he goes to trial. He's got a wife and three-year-old son, so there's a deal to be made I believe."

"How would we go about it, that is, if we did it?" Reid said questioningly.

"We need to get him aside at the Remand Section. We

need to strike a deal with him, but he will have to get his solicitor to try for bail. He will have to do that by himself because we don't want to be seen anywhere near his solicitor. He's got to put out that it is his idea because it could be months before he comes up for trial and he has a three-year-old at home. He'll put up his passport and even though Vulpe would be surprised if he got bail, Funan is his right-hand man, and he needs him out. If we say that we may not have the cases ready for months, then the Magistrate has to take that into account."

"What about his mate Dalca?" Max Tyler chipped in.

"If we only put up that we want Funan's passport and a decent surety and he makes bail, I'm sure that Vulpe and his legal team will soon line up again for Dalca," Signorotto replied.

"That would mean we are back to square one with all three out on the streets," Anderson said.

"Yes and no," Signorotto said. "If we have Funan turned, that leaves Vulpe by himself really. Dalca is just a puppet. He'll do as he's told by Funan. We want to know how Vulpe is bringing in and distributing the drugs, but we also want to keep an eye on him because of the threats to the judge and to you also, ma'am."

"He hasn't actually made any threat against me Tony," Reid said.

"Ma'am, with respect. I know the types that live around these inner suburbs because I've grown up here and lived my whole life near these scumbags. You have massively disrespected him with the shoe bit. You are a female in uniform and a high up member of the police force. That's three strikes you're out as far as he's concerned. Take my word on it, he will want back at you and that will be uppermost in his mind. First the judge sentencing his main distributor then you. He'll want to get back against the establishment before his trial comes up. He's one mad Romanian is our Bogdan Vulpe."

"What's your suggestion going forward, Senior Sergeant?" The Deputy Commissioner asked.

"If we get a meeting with Funan as quick as possible and get him up for bail within, say, a week and if it goes all right, I think that within two weeks we can have them all back together on the streets. Max and I can run Funan, but the Prosecution Department will have to cut a very good deal with him. If he's going to do this, I think we'll have to stump up for him and his family to go into Witness Protection to get away from Vulpe's clutches," Signorotto said.

"That can all be done, I believe," said the Deputy Commissioner. "Vulpe might only get a year or two for the threats to kill against Cel Tradat, but if we can put him up on large scale drug importation charges, with Funan's help, we can get him twenty or thirty years. At the same time that he is supplying you with information, though, I am very worried about Vulpe and his obsession with revenge, especially against the judiciary and the police department. He might lay low for a while, but once his cohorts are out, I want round the clock protection for Justice Wilson and for Superintendent Reid. Inspector Anderson, I'll leave that to you. I'll authorise plain clothes Force Response members to be at your disposal twenty-four seven."

"Deputy Commissioner, do you think it is necessary that I have round the clock protection?" Reid said with a note of disdain in her voice.

"Superintendent. When you return to London at some stage, I want you to go back for a visit, not to be the centre of attention at a funeral. In the meantime, and until we get

Vulpe on some big charges, Senior Constable Schaeffer here can be assigned as your driver. I'll lend Carlton another member to cover her position. Right, let's get this started. I want reports back to me regularly, thank you people," he said, rising from the table.

Chapter 13

Anton Funan didn't know why he had been placed in an interview room at the Remand prison. He was sitting on a chair which was bolted to the concrete floor behind a small table in the centre of the windowless and airless room. His hands were cuffed in front of him, but they had also been secured with a chain that ran under a steel bar that was connected to the table. The great escape artist Houdini would have struggled to free himself, which there was no point in attempting to do as one of the walls contained a large viewing glass window which allowed those on the other side to see in, but never for the prisoner to view out. There was only one thing to do and that was to sit tight and see who would walk through the door. Days had passed since the bail hearings for himself, and Codrin Dalca, which had been unsuccessful, so he was a bit surprised that a lawyer hadn't been sent from Vulpe to make an attempt for bail again.

He knew his star was on the wane with the Romanian since he had spoken back to him when it became obvious that Vulpe was getting more and more agitated because other mafiosi steered clear of the Romanian ever since he had upset the apple cart by putting pressure on a female staffer at Geelong prison to threaten a prisoner. The word had gone back down the line that Vulpe was a coward. Various thoughts were spinning around in his head when the door suddenly burst open. Funan recognised Tony Signorotto immediately, even though the burly looking police office was in a suit this time and not a uniform. The other one he didn't know by name, but he recognised him from the raid at the cleaning headquarters. Both sat down opposite him. Rather than feeling intimidated or scared, Funan felt a flutter of hope. He didn't want to spend the next ten years or so in prison.

"Anton, you know who I am. My name is Senior Sergeant Tony Signorotto, and this is Detective Sergeant Max Tyler," he said indicating to his left where Max was seated. "We don't want to be here long because the longer we stay, the more the word might get out that we have been talking to you."

"What are you after?" a nervous Funan replied.

"I am going to cut to the chase, Anton. I am involved in this now because you and your mate did the unbelievably stupid thing of threatening a Supreme Court judge who happens to live on my patch. He is upset and I am upset, and that is not good. Add to that the fact that you have been raided and caught with a firearm leaves you with a lot of problems."

"You haven't come here to tell me stuff that I already know. Again, what are you after?"

"It's not what we're after, Anton. We can let you slide quite easily into the prison system, which is in fact what you really deserve for what you've been doing, shifting drugs for Vulpe. You need to think of some way you can save yourself. I mean it would make sense seeing that you have a wife and son," Max Tyler stated clearly. "We're not going to fuck around here playing twenty questions pal, so wake up to yourself. Why do you think we are here?"

"How do I get myself out of this mess? What do you want me to do, because whatever it is it will be the end of me with Vulpe and his Romanian connections. I'd be signing my own death sentence unless you have some sort of plan for me and my family."

"You've brought it up so obviously you are interested in

some sort of deal. Is that correct?" Signorotto said looking Funan directly in the eye.

Anton Funan flicked his eyes from one member to the other and back again for what seemed like an eternity to Signorotto before finally speaking in a whisper.

"Are you recording this?"

"No Anton, we're not," Tyler said.

"Okay, I'll deal, but you are going to have to protect me and my family—and not here in Melbourne!"

"We need you to apply for bail again, Anton." Signorotto said. "This time though, we won't put up a real fight against it. We will be telling the bench that we won't have the cases against you and Dalca ready for months. Obviously, we will ask for your passports to be handed in but what we want is you back around Vulpe and feeding us information."

"Are you talking both of us?"

"You need to get in touch with your legal team and Vulpe and say that we have been back here for an interview with you, and we let it slip that your trials won't be coming up for months and you want another crack at bail. They should handle the rest. They will be successful because you won't be going up in front of the same Magistrate again," Tyler chipped in.

"Vulpe will get her again, that's a given," Funan said.

"No, the system won't allow the Magistrate who denied you bail to sit on your second hearing. You know and we know that she was only interested in getting Vulpe bail. Leave the Magistrate question with us," Signorotto said emphatically.

"So, you're trying to get us both out on bail?"

"The Magistrate will have to give you both bail. Don't you worry about it. We will then be in touch with you, okay?" Tyler said.

"Fine, I get out on bail with a heap of charges still to face and you want me to fizz on Vulpe. What do I get in return? Not much good getting off charges if he finds out I've grassed. He'll just kill me," a wide-eyed Funan replied.

"As soon as we have enough on him and his business, you and your family will be going into the Witness Protection scheme and then re-located. Where, will be up to you. Your charges will disappear, and you will have a new life, but first we have to get Vulpe put away. Consider yourself fortunate that we are asking you seeing that you have helped him with the importation of drugs over the years. We want the snake's head, not the body."

"What about Dalca. Where does he fit in?"

"He doesn't. He gets bail and just goes back to work. You tell him nothing. This is only a deal for you. In your interview when you got arrested, you made it pretty clear that you thought Vulpe was getting out of hand, and you wanted out. Well, this is out in a big way. A one-off deal which you either say yes to now or we walk, and you wait in here then go to trial and just change cells afterwards. You are looking at ten years at the moment, so what's it to be Anton? Help us and you help your family. Simple as that," Signorotto said as he stood and turned towards the door with Tyler.

"It's a deal," Funan said as he tried to stand but couldn't because of his restraints

"No doubt we will be hearing from your legal team. The ball's in your court, excuse the pun," Signorotto said with a slight smile on his face.

Chapter 14

"Kate, do you think that with your 'foot in the door' so to speak with His Honour Miles Wilson that you could possibly speak to him about the Magistrate situation for when Funan and Dalca come up again? You told us that he is a wake-up to Vulpe's influence on that last Magistrate, Alexa Mitrea," Superintendent Anne Reid said to her Task Force meeting.

"I can give it a try. He was furious about the run-around she gave him with the original bail hearing, and from a message he sent me a couple of days ago, I can tell you that Mitrea has now been assigned to the Western District court circuit for the next three years. I think she'll be dealing with cattle and sheep stealing for quite some time. Also, a drop in pay seeing that the court lists down there aren't quite as long as up here. Silly girl should have checked the top court list for which judges move the little minnows around. Bad mistake. What do you want me to ask him?"

"As we all know, Anton Funan is about to apply for another bail hearing. From the phone register at the Remand Centre, we have been told he has made a few phone calls in the last two days. There was at least two going to Bogdan Vulpe and then there was one to the same solicitor's firm that did the last bail hearing for Vulpe and then two came back from them. What we need to do is have a Magistrate that will basically go along with the wishes of Miles Wilson. We need him back out if we want to bring down Vulpe."

"If you want to carry on with the rest of the meeting, I'll give his house a ring now. It's a Saturday so he won't be in court. He is very pro police and has a brother-in-law that is a Senior Sergeant. See how I go," Kate replied as she stood and walked into a nearby office and rang Wilson's number.

"Your Honour, Kate McLaren here," she said when the phone was answered.

"Kate, I've told you that if it's not in court then it's Miles. What can I do to assist you?"

"Miles, you know all about our determination to get the drugs off the streets that Bogdan Vulpe is flooding them with at the moment, well we have a situation where his two associates are applying for bail and to be honest, we need Anton Funan back out there. He is doing a deal with the Justice Department for himself and his family to stay out of gaol and get out from under Vulpe."

There was silence from the other end of the phone and Kate McLaren imagined the wheels that were turning in the judge's mind. After about ten seconds he replied.

"If I can help in any way to keep the drugs off the streets then I'll do what I can. Reading between the lines you want a favourable Magistrate on the bench, is that it?"

"In a nutshell, yes, we do. We believe that with the information that Funan can get back to us we can add large scale drug supplying to Vulpe's upcoming charges of threats to kill Cel Tradat at Barwon. We want to bring his whole operation down and we need an inside informer."

"Have you heard of a Magistrate by the name of Simon Colpin?" Wilson said slowly.

"No, I haven't, Miles. I take it you know him?"

"I know all the Magistrates, Kate. I'll see him tomorrow night at dinner and you'll see him whenever that bail hearing takes place. Enough said?"

"Miles, I understand, but also, with that madman Vulpe free and back with his cronies, I am going to get onto the

Force Response Unit and have them monitor your house and family. I won't have any arguments about that. Vulpe, according to Funan in his interview, has vowed revenge not just with you but also now after a situation with one of our Superintendents it looks like he's gunning for us as well. Some of us think he's been sampling a bit too much of his own illegal proiduct, if you know what I mean. We have to get him back behind bars with some decent charges and then he can rot there till he comes up before a higher court."

"Thanks Kate. Obviously, we never had this conversation, and I would trust you not to reveal it. I'm sure you have ways of communicating with a nudge and a wink. I've seen how you lot operate in court," Wilson said with a laugh before ending the call.

Kate McLaren returned to the meeting and took her seat. When she looked up at several members she spoke.

"Why are you all looking at me?"

"Did you do any good?" Vince Anderson said.

Kate replied with a wink towards him. "Don't ask."

"Right then," Reid said. "Vince, Tony, how do you think we should run this?"

"Well," Anderson replied," there are several layers to this. First and foremost is giving Funan easy access to someone in the Task Force when he wants to give us information. Seeing that Tony has been dealing with him, I suggest that he is the conduit with him either by phone or in person somewhere. What do you think, Tony?"

"I reckon that would be best. He's used to me and if I can't meet or talk to him for some reason, then he has met Max and he can do it also."

"That's one task," Anderson continued. "I have applied for and been granted a continuous phone tap on Vulpe's office phone, his mobile and his home phone. Through the District Response Unit, we are going to be running a round the clock monitor of his phones once Funan gets out on bail, which hopefully will be sometime next week. We want to see what Vulpe does or says especially in regard to Judge Wilson and you also, Superintendent," Anderson said turning to Reid. "I want to supply you with a driver until this comes to a head, so I have arranged for your plain car to be swapped over at the Traffic Branch for the time being. You are going to have a Leading Senior Constable form the Melbourne Highway Patrol driving you everywhere, including picking you up and dropping you at home. You'll be in one of their unmarked BMW's for the time being. Chloe Schaeffer will be your liaison member, Superintendent. This will also start next week. Last but not least is a twenty-four seven sit-off of Judge Wilson and his family. He will be looked after at court by senior PSO's who will meet him at his car and take him back to his car at the end of the day. Kate, you will continue to be his liaison person. He will also have a Highway Patrol member driving one of the Traffic Branch's BMW's. The Force Response Unit will keep a watch on his house. I'll get both drivers' names for you soon so you can contact them. I'm not going to take any chances with this. Vulpe will be out for some sort of revenge wherever he can. He's used to having his own way."

Superintendent Reid looked around the members at the table. "Well, next thing is the bail hearing which we should be notified about soon. I want all members fully armed and equipped from here on in. I must admit I didn't expect the reaction I got back from Vulpe when I did what I did. Let's see how far he wants to go."

"Some of my Italian contacts around Carlton and Fitzroy

have already contacted me, ma'am, and they are saying he's as mad as a cut snake over the court situation where Cel Tradat was given time and also your action."

"Don't keep bringing up that show episode, Senior Sergeant., I'll do what I have to do with these types and I won't be lectured by you," a stern sounding Reid said quite loudly.

Tony Signorotto just stared back at her.

Your arrogance will be your downfall, lady, he thought to himself.

Chapter 15

Bogdan Vulpe sat one row back in the Melbourne Magistrates court number three. Long before the presiding Magistrate, Simon Colpin entered, the prosecutor together with Tony Signorotto and Max Tyler had been staring at the show that Vulpe had put on with members of his legal team. He was furious and he didn't care who heard him.

"What the fuck do you mean Mitrea's not available? This was meant to be fixed. I'm not here to listen to some clown that doesn't owe me favours. Funan could end up back in remand and that's not what I'm paying you for. I want him out, understand you morons?"

"Codrin Dalca is also up for a bail hearing also, Mr Vulpe," came the reply from Vulpe's barrister.

"I don't give a fuck about Dalca. I need Funan back out to run my cleaning business," Vulpe lied. "Where's my beak? Why isn't she sitting?"

Vulpe's very nervous barrister gave the answer that sent his client into a rage.

"The senior court judges have reviewed the list of Magistrates and decided to send her to the Western District for a few years. Apparently one of them wasn't happy with her decision about letting you out on bail whilst keeping Mr. Dalcan and Mr. Funan in gaol awaiting trial."

In the near empty courtroom, Vulpe grabbed a sheath of papers from the defence barrister's table and slammed them down so hard they cascaded like an avalanche onto the floor causing them to slide across the court room towards the Magistrates bench. He screamed at his defence team.

"I own her. She's fucking mine," the reply came in an

almost demented sounding voice.

His barrister and junior solicitor quickly moved their chairs away from Vulpe as they buried their heads in the paperwork of the bail applications.

"I wonder what he will make of us not putting up much of a fight to keep them in remand?" Tony whispered to Max.

"This bloke thinks he can just buy everyone and everything, no matter who or what. He's mad," Max said just as Simon Colpin stepped out to sit at the bench. He looked down at the papers spread across the floor and spoke.

"A little misunderstanding at the defence table, gentlemen? I'll give you a minute or so to clean up before we proceed," he said with a knowing grin on his face.

The junior solicitor scooted around from the defence table, got down on hands and knees and quickly picked up the loose sheaths after which the defence barrister nodded his thanks to Colpin.

"Right, gentlemen. Let the proceedings begin," he indicated to the defence table.

After ten minutes of grovelling from Vulpe's team, their barrister resumed his seat slowly as the Crown Prosecutor rose from his.

"Your Worship, the Prosecution concedes that the two defendants in these cases may face an unwarranted time on Remand. The higher court lists are longer than was first thought and the preparation time for the briefs of evidence may be held up due to security arrangements for one of the witnesses. The Department of Public Prosecutions wants to ensure the long-term safety of a star witness in the case against the defendant Bogdan Vulpe who, as you can see, is sitting behind the legal team for the defence," the

Prosecutor stated.

Vulpe's face reddened as he went to rise behind his barrister. The assisting solicitor turned immediately and very sternly insisted he sit down and remain seated.

"What is the security issue that could delay the trials for Vulpe and his two accused?" Colpin asked the Prosecutor, knowing full well the answer he was going to receive.

"It surrounds layers of security for our witness. This is the witness Bogdan Vulpe threatened regarding Chiral Cel Tradat, who is now deceased."

Vulpe exploded off his seat with a tirade of abusive language towards the Prosecutor.

"Remove yourself from this court immediately Mr. Vulpe. This hearing is not about you but two of your associates. One word from you on your way out and you'll be headed down to the cells with your own bail revoked," Colpin said pointing the fuming Romanian towards the exit.

Vulpe turned on his heels and glared at the Prosecutor as he exited the courtroom.

"My sincere apologies, Your Worship," the defence barrister said.

"Not your fault, but I wonder sometimes if it is worth taking a retainer from someone like Vulpe? The money must be big, but it does your reputation no good at all. Now Mr. Prosecutor, please continue," Colpin said.

"Yes, well, as I was going to say, Your Worship, if the trials are going to be delayed, it will only mean more appearances back here for bail applications. We are asking for a ten-thousand-dollar security for both Codrin Dalca and Anton Funan and their passports to be handed in. Twice weekly attendances at the Fitzroy police station as well, if you please."

The defence solicitor quickly turned to his senior

barrister and whispered.

"This is a surprise. I thought they would fight the applications tooth and nail."

"Very much of a surprise, but why didn't they apply for a condition that the three of the defendants stay away from each other? I smell a rat here, but I can't say anything against it. This application is five thousand dollars in our firm's bank if I get them bail."

"I accept those conditions Your Worship. I will inform Mr. Vulpe outside to get the twenty thousand dollars transferred into the court's legal fund."

"The two bail applicants won't be released until that money is in," Colpin said. "Does that satisfy the Prosecution?"

The Prosecutor turned and feigned a conversation with Signorotto and Tyler before turning back to Collins and nodding his head in agreeance.

"Very well then, once the twenty thousand dollars is in the court's account, they will both be released. Also, please tell your Mr. Vulpe that he came within a whisker of losing his bail. If he puts on a circus act like that in the top court, I can guarantee you that he will be removed from the court forcibly. I won't put up with that rubbish in my court and I'm sure a top court judge won't either," Colpin said with a seriously.

The defence barrister rose and acknowledged Colpin's words.

All rose as the Colpin exited the court through a door behind his seat. Signorotto leant towards the red-faced defence barrister and spoke.

"A spit-the-dummy performance of the top order by one of your clients, eh?"

The barrister put his head down next to Signorotto's and

replied quietly.

"I trust you to keep this to yourselves, Senior Sergeant, but I think I can read a plan of attack as well as the next barrister and let me assure you of two things. First of all, I will not be divulging my thoughts to Vulpe regarding your thoughts on bail and secondly, once his fee for today hits our trust fund it will be the last time we have anything to do with him. Our company's reputation is far more important than he. Have a good day," he said gathering his files and handing the whole box to his junior brief as he turned to the door.

Chapter 16

For now, Anton Funan had no intention of telling his wife why he was out on bail. Things would change, of course, when the time came for him to tell her exactly how he was going to remain out of gaol.

His wife had no idea that he was a player in the Melbourne drugs scene. She believed that Funan was the general manager of the Cleanstyle Industrial Cleaning Company and what had happened to lock him up was the result of the police fitting him up because he happened to work for Bogdan Vulpe. She believed that he was a doting father of a little boy and had to work very odd hours to make the company competitive in today's market. Never did she realise that ninety per cent of his work was nothing to do with industrial cleaning of buildings, but more the industrial cleaning of drugs and money. She lived in her own blissful little world and looked after the family home.

For his part, Anton Funan was trying to live in two worlds, and neither of them were blissful. He was back taking orders from Vulpe and sorting out what the Task Force wanted to hear and how he could get it to them. For the previous two weeks he had been taking photos of various substances that were coming in and going out of the cleaning factory. The trouble was none of the markings were incriminating. He would have to get proof of contacts who picked the substances up and saw what was inside the packaging. The only other way was to get Vulpe on tape talking about where they came from and what different types of drugs they were. He had noticed though, that one large crate marked as an industrial floor cleaning machine, which had arrived two days previous, was still sitting at the back of the factory. He always knew what came in and out, but this crate was a mystery. If he was to remain across everything, he had to know the contents.

"Boss, that crate down the back marked as an industrial cleaning machine. I don't know anything about it. Who's it for?"

"We're moving up a gear in the field, Anton," Vulpe said. Oxycontin, Xanax and Adderall are huge now in the States. What we have in that crate is a shipment of Fentanyl. Came in through a bikie contact in Romania who is the President of the Black Knights over there. I want a distribution set up where we can supply fentanyl, cocaine and heroin all together. Our clients can use it how they please. Some areas down south in America can't get enough Oxycontin. It's a huge area which is mainly untouched here is Australia. I want to be on top of the market with this."

"Boss, if that came in through your Romanian contacts with the Black Knights, don't you think you should set up a meet with the Chapter of the Black Knights here? They'll know there's shit being sent over and the Romanians will want you to distribute through them, I'd say," Funan said cautiously.

"It's between my contact and me, nothing to do with their guys here. I want you to work on all this. I have a couple of loose ends to tie up in the legal world first," Vulpe said with a vicious looking grin on his face.

Funan didn't know which question to ask first. Was it going to be about not wanting to be head of distribution where he knew for sure he would be upsetting a bikie gang? He would be signing his own death warrant there. First off though he realised he had to get some information about 'the loose ends in the legal world' statement.

"Got a nasty letter from your law firm?" he said trying to

give a small laugh at the same time.

"Paid their bill for your bail application, then get a 'please fuck off' letter from them. They'll keep. No, I have a couple of scores to settle with that fucking judge and that bitch Superintendent," an angry Vulpe said.

"Boss don't want to interfere, but if you are going to start dealing in Fentanyl, which is pretty new to here, I'd reckon I'd be steering well clear of the law. Don't want to fight them on two fronts. Why don't we just concentrate on what we know? The pre-cursors for supplying drug labs is getting us heaps. The benzaldehyde and ephedrine we are shipping is what we are good at."

Vulpe gave Funan a questioning look before he spoke.

"Listen, I didn't get you out on bail so you can just carry on as before. I could have Dalca do that. You are going to head up the fentanyl distribution. I want new markets and I don't want bikies involved. I want to get into the professional world. Doctors, lawyers and all sorts of professionals over in the States are hooked on this stuff. That's what I want here. I want you to really get this up and running. You'll get a bigger pay cheque and, like I said, Dalca can carry on with the day to day running of the company and the ins and outs to the warehouse for our normal street trade. I've got a few upmarket company contacts who tell me their high-flying mates are getting bored with a line of coke and want to push life along a little bit quicker. He reckons if we get onto them, they live their nights in the city's hotspots for the wealthy. We'll sit down this afternoon, and I'll get you the numbers of who you should start with," Vulpe said as he stood and headed into the office area.

"Do you want me to help with the legal bit? A bit of warning to the judge?" Funan said quickly, trying to get the conversation back to what he had to find out. The fentanyl bit would be a big plus to get Vulpe back behind bars, but he had a feeling he wanted to save face with the law first. At this stage, he could deny everything about the shipment and maybe just wanted to see what heat came down on his employee. Fentanyl wasn't big in Australia, but Funan would bet the Feds would be all over him if he started to make inquiries to off-load twenty kilos of it.

"If I need you, I'll call you. Talk after lunch about the machinery down the back."

Anton Funan walked towards the crate at the back of the warehouse thinking to himself.

He's serious about revenge if he's got that judge and copper in the gun and lets me deal with the fentanyl. That's big money and the other shit is big trouble.

Chapter 17

Anton Funan arranged to meet Tony Signorotto and Max Tyler behind the old grandstand at the Brunswick Street oval, the former home of the VFL Fitzroy Football Club whose name had been morphed into the Brisbane Bears and then the Brisbane Lions. He had a lot to tell them.

Tony Signorotto had spent his life around Carlton, Fitzroy and Collingwood and it showed in his choice of cars. His drive was a 1972 John Goss Ford Falcon V8, green over white. It was his pride and joy and he had parked it carefully behind the grandstand. Funan was going to have to walk to him. Signorotto was not going to leave his chariot to the whims of some spaced-out junkie to try to break into. He admitted to Tyler that it was a good place for a meet, because the only people who would be over this way late at night would probably recognise the familiar face of the big Senior Sergeant and take off quick smart.

Funan appeared out of the darkness and approached the two men. There were no handshakes, just quick nods.

"You got some good intel for us, Funan?" Max Tyler said first off.

"Two things, and you're not going to like either. First off, Vulpe has basically promoted me while he thinks of ways to get back at that judge and your lady boss. He's not going to let it go I can tell you straight up."

"Anything specific or just vague innuendos?" Signorotto replied.

"Not yet, but I know him well enough to tell you it won't be anything insignificant and most likely the coward will try and get Dalca and some others onto it."

"Why not you? You're his main man. Surely there's a risk

of something going wrong sending that idiot Dalca to do his work for him?"

"Dalca would do anything he says without question and when it all goes pear-shaped, he'd take the full blame. He worships the little prick. Vulpe will leave him high and dry. Dalca's family will be looked after no matter what happens but as of now, I don't know what his plans are, but in a day or so I'm going to sound out Dalca on the quiet. The other thing is that with this so-called promotion it has just put me in the firing line for sure. You won't believe what this guy wants to get into."

"We know he deals and imports drugs, that's why we're giving you the chance to bust him open. You must know shipment dates and other stuff?" Tyler said with an inquisitive look.

"He's basically put Dalca in charge of that. Now, would you believe, he is importing fentanyl. There's a crate down the back of the warehouse that is marked as cleaning machinery. It's machinery all right but it's full of fentanyl. He got it from some bikie in Romania and now wants me to head up the distribution of it here in Melbourne."

Signorotto stared at Tyler with an alarmed look.

"Fentanyl?" Signorotto said virtually spitting out the word." Even the hard-core mafia around town aren't touching that stuff yet until they have a proper supply chain from the States. My contacts tell me that it's certainly on the cards down the track, but none of them want to be the guinea pig who's first up to court for being nabbed dealing in it. It's wrecking homes and families by the minute in the southern states of the USA, but no one here trusts any of the madmen who want to supply it. You say some Romanian bikie is sending it over?" a clearly disturbed Signorotto said.

"Yeah. He's the President of the Black Knights over there. I did some digging on them and they even have all the other groups on the backfoot when it comes to supply," Funan said.

"The others aren't stupid," Tyler said. "It's like not buying the first model of a car. Wait for the second model and a lot of the bugs will have been fixed. They'll let the Feds take the pickings and the bottom-feeders will die out."

"He's setting you up for a big fall, Anton," Signorotto said. "Maybe on purpose or maybe it's just greed. He's thinking that you'll stuff up on your first dealings and then he can blame you and throw you to the wolves if it fucks up, and as sure as God made little green apples, it will once the Feds get wind of it. Jesus, fentanyl! Makes smack look like a party drug. It gets disguised as Oxycontin and other things and it's deadly."

"Well, he's given me a list of people around town I can distribute to, but I reckon the bikie gangs here will want to be top of the list for distribution when they hear, but he wants me to deal with his list people first. The Melbourne chapter of the Black Knights aren't necessarily all Romanian, but they have their roots back there and they will want their share before anyone else. Vulpe's taking a big risk I think, and I don't want to be the front man when the locals get kick off about the distribution chain rights."

"How long can you stall him and keep the stuff at your factory?" Tyler said. "If you play a few of his contacts off against each other with prices and such, we may have a way in. Can't tell you how but things could get stirred up over a few weeks which might set the bikies against Vulpe, especially if they want the stuff and you can't get a deal done anywhere else. He can't afford to keep the stuff at his own premises. Too risky if word gets out that there is a bit of a conflict about who is wanting the stuff. We could easily get a raid done and make it look like we got the information from a source somewhere else. We need to let it simmer for a few weeks and make it look like you've got warring factions who keep upping the price. Vulpe's greed is well known, so he'll let them go back and forth for at least a week. By that stage we can get the bikies involved if their noses are out of joint."

"I can't let anyone on the list know that I'm playing them off against each other. That will get them pissed off and me killed. Two weeks max," Funan said cautiously.

"If you tell him you've put out feelers and that the bids are going up, then that will give him a bit of space to plot his pathetic revenge bit. We're going to have to know constantly how the bidding war is going. Are any of the other parties going to go to him about you saying the bids are going up every day?" Signorotto said.

"No, these guys know he always deals through a third party. He never gets caught in the web. Always blokes like me that they must deal with. I already know one or two on the list, so I can start with them. Should all stay calm for the first week before the Black Knights want their share.

"Now we know about the fentanyl, we could go in straight away with a warrant but that would put you under the spotlight. Vulpe would smell a rat. By giving you some time, it gives him time for the revenge plan. You're going to have to let us know immediately if he sets his dogs loose onto the judge or the superintendent though. You a chance at all to find out plans or will he just go in with himself and Dalca and others?" Max said.

"My bet is he'll plan it then use Dalca. Vulpe thinks he himself is untouchable. Thinks he's King of Romania here in Melbourne," Funan said.

"Okay but keep us updated daily. You've got our numbers and I presume you are using a burner?" Max Tyler said.

"Yep," a worried looking Funan said before turning to leave the meeting. "This better work out for me. I'm putting my head on the block for this, understand?"

"Understood," Tyler said as they walked to Signorotto's car. "It's a pity that we have to divide our team into three separate areas, but we need to make the fentanyl the priority, eh, Tony?"

"For sure, but tell the judge or the superintendent that," the big Senior Sergeant said looking over the roof of his car at Tyler before sliding into the driver's seat of the big V8.

Chapter 18

If nothing else, Bogdan Vulpe was cunning. Revenge would be sweet and would be made even sweeter when it was delivered through unexpected channels. He also wasn't a person to procrastinate. One of the ideas he would handle himself, through the family. The other would take a large wad of cash not only for payment to the person he would pick for the job but also for the supplies needed. Explosives didn't come cheap.

Reaching into his desk drawer, he picked out one of his many burner phones and punched in the number of a contact he was keeping for a rainy day. His name was Florin Barbu, a former member of the *Romanian Brigada 6 Operati Speciale*, the anti-terrorist wing of the Romanian armed forces. Now a resident of Melbourne for over ten years, his reputation preceded him regarding demolition jobs. He was not a standover merchant, just a specialist in his field. He had done a few small jobs for Vulpe over the last few years where customers who refused to pay or were late in paying for their deliveries soon found out that their means of transport had disappeared in a fiery ball in front of their workplace or home. He would never take on a job where it meant someone could be hurt or killed. Those times were past. The destruction of property was what he excelled in.

"Florin, how are you, my friend? Bogdan Vulpe here. A while since we have spoken."

"You paid your account. The job was done, and the money delivered. No need for us to see each other." Barbu said flatly.

"Absolutely Florin. I have another one if you're

interested. Different type of transportation this time. It's a yacht."

"What type of yacht? Fibreglass, steel. I need specifics," Barbu said cutting to the chase.

"All I know is that it is named '*Legal Eagle*' and it sits at the Brighton Yacht Club. There's twenty-five thousand in it for you if it goes to the bottom but I want it done this week," an impatient Vulpe said.

"If you know it is at Brighton, I need the berth number so I can get in there to see what needs to be done. I take it there is no-one living on it?"

"I have an interest in the security company that looks after the marina, so I will give you the details tonight. No one is on board, and it hasn't been used for months. Do we have a deal?" Vulpe said.

"I don't know what I need yet so it will be thirty thousand and five thousand for the C9, which I will get. That's my deal. Payment all needs to be done this week cash, by tomorrow afternoon. If it's all good, then the job will be done."

"You drive a hard bargain, Florin, but yes, that will be paid. Where?"

"Outside Luna Park tomorrow at one. After that, no more contact."

"One of my associates will deliver the money tomorrow. He'll be wearing a green jacket and white shoes. You won't miss him."

"More to the point, he'd better not miss me. No cash, no job," Barbu said.

"When the job is done, I will get you to lay a special wreath on the site," Vulpe said, ending the call. He then pulled the back of the mobile phone he was using, removed the SIM card and threw it into the large glass ashtray on his desk. After lighting another Romanian Carpati cigarette, he took the Bic lighter and held it to the SIM card until it had melted into the ashtray. He then took another burner phone from the desk and proceeded to dial a number in London. A few seconds passed before he spoke.

"*Buna dimineta*," he said knowing it was early morning in London. There was a prolonged silence at the other end before he heard a voice.

"Good morning to you too," was the reply from the weaselly sounding voice of Mercia Vulpe, first cousin to Bogdan. "This must be a business call seeing that it is early morning here and I didn't recognise the number. What do you want, dear cousin Bogdan?"

"I have a superintendent of the state police here that decided not only to arrest me for nothing days ago but at the end of our conversation, wiped her shoe on my chest. She is a temporary transfer member to Victoria and has come by courtesy of your metropolitan Police in London. I will not be insulted by anyone, let alone a female cop in this manner so I have decided a little pay back is in order. You follow so far?"

"I take it she didn't stand on a bench and wipe her shoe on you. My guess is that you were in a prone position, handcuffed and spiting at her, if I know you at all cousin," Mercia said with the satisfaction that there were thousands of kilometres between the two of them. Bogdan took no notice of the pointed return.

"I will send you details of where her parents live outside London. It's amazing what these idiots will say in an interview. I have all her details from a copy of Police Life magazine. I don't want anything done to her parents, just a particular wreath laid outside their front door with a note with a special message."

"When do you want it done?"

"Late one evening this week. I'll give you all the details of the job via the encrypted App, and make sure it's done in cash through one of our funeral services there."

"Send it to me and I'll see what I can do."

"No talking, nothing at all except for the wreath, understand? Just need to send her a message. Being one of the Brotherhood, I need this job done quickly, as in ASAP."

"What's in it for me?" Mercia said with a sleepy but irritated voice.

"My gratitude and your continued good health, little cousin," the gravelly answer came back.

Mercia made no reply. It was family and he knew family would mean nothing to Bogdan if the job wasn't done correctly and on time.

Chapter 19

Florin Barbu had been found by Vulpe's contact the next day as planned outside Luna Park in St. Kilda. No words were exchanged, and the two strangers passed like two ships in the night albeit for a five second deposit of a large, heavy camp style backpack into Barbu's outstretched hand after which he walked another two blocks before he found a quiet, secluded spot to sit on foreshore where he removed and counted the thirty-five thousand dollars. He had demanded the extra five thousand to buy the explosives but that would just go to himself as he already had a cache of the required material safely packed away in the ceiling of his house. Also in the package was a piece of paper showing details of the yacht, *Legal Eagle* which he saw was at a pontoon mooring not far inside the boundary of the Brighton Yacht Club. There was also a hand drawn map of where to scale the fence so as to avoid any CCTV cameras.

He lifted the pack onto his back and walked to his Balaclava house, where he found a wreath adorned with a dozen black roses and a typed note which read, '*To be left as a calling card.*' Florin Barbu neither knew nor cared what the significance of the wreath meant but with his fee and information in hand he planned on completing the contract that night. He went to bed, set his phone alarm for one o'clock the next morning and went to sleep.

Upon wakening, he dressed completely in black, including black rubber gloves, removed the small canister of C9 from the ceiling and placed it and the required wiring in a Safeway bag. On top of his 'tools of trade' he placed some lightweight groceries to cover everything. He then carried the bag and the wreath outside to his very unobtrusive Ford Focus and drove towards the Brighton Yacht Club.

Parking in Grosvenor Street near a closed shop opposite the club, he waited another hour before getting out of the car with the package and wreath. Crossing the Esplanade quickly, he tossed the wreath over the fence, put his arm through the handles of the Safeway bag and in two grabs, scaled the fence. Forty metres later he was beside his target which was riding quietly at its mooring pontoon. He wasted no time getting on board to check there was no person sleeping rough in the expensive boat. He then attached a timer to the water tight package and placed the magnetised cannister just under the metal transom. The last thing Barbu did was to release the halyard and tie the wreath to it. He then raised it up the mast, leaving enough slack in the halyard so that when the yacht sank the wreath would be visible floating on the surface. He was back over the fence and in his car within minutes. Quietly driving away from his parking spot, he heard a muffled *woomph* which satisfied him that *Legal Eagle* would be quietly settling in water to within about two metres of the top of its mast.

He was satisfied with the job, the money and the fact that the damage was to property only. As for Bogdan Vulpe knowing his address, he wasn't worried. Vulpe knew quite well that if any sort of trail led back to his house or himself, he would be dead within days. The *Romanian Brigada 6 Oprati Speciale* had long and deadly tentacles. The Romanian mafia wasn't the only Brotherhood in the world.

***

On the other side of the world, in the quiet country village of Cobham in the Borough of Elmbridge in Surrey, just seventeen miles from London, Irene and Geoff Reid were settling down for a late cup of tea in their thatched centuries old cottage when Geoff turned to Irene and spoke.

"Was that the front door bell, luv?"

Irene Reid nodded to him but said nothing as she quietly went to the front door and opened it. She looked out into the now greying evening and the deserted laneway and the fields beyond. Not seeing any sign of a visitor, she was turning back to close the door when she looked down and saw circular wreath lying to one side of the doorway. She took two steps and bent down to see that it was made up of a display of black roses. She called for her husband.

"Geoff, luv. There's flowers at door. You haven't gone and bought flowers for me, have ya?" she laughed as he turned on the hallway light and then picked up the wreath to examine it.

"There's a card," he said. "I didn't send this. If I'd done, it would have been red uns, not black and not a bloody wreath."

"Read it," a slightly shaken Irene said.

"*Best of health to Irene, Geoff and Anne,*" Geoff read. "Anne lives in Australia, and what about our other two, Peter and Margaret. What's this about?"

"Got no idea, luv, but it's got me a bit shaky, them roses being black and all. Have ya tea and give young Anne a call. She might be able to help. Looks like a funeral wreath or such," Irene said before closing the door and pulling her cardigan tightly around herself more for security than warmth as Geoff placed the wreath just inside on the hallstand.

"Aye, luv. I'll make a phone call to her," a confused Geoff said before reaching for the teapot.

Chapter 20

It was just after seven o'clock in the morning when Anne Reid's desk phone rang.

At that time of the morning, she realised it would be either urgent or bad news of some sort. No one usually rang any of the headquarter's Superintendents or above before they had attended 'prayers' on the top floor with the Chief without a very good reason. 'Prayers' were scheduled for seven-thirty.

"Superintendent Reid," she said cautiously before letting her face break into a broad smile as she heard the home country accent of her father, Geoff. "Do you realise what time it is here?" she said with a laugh.

"Wouldn't ring if it weren't important, luv," he said. Got a bit of a surprise here at the door and it has your name on it."

Ten minutes later, Anne Reid put the phone back in its cradle but sat there with her hand still on it. The story was certainly strange, but she couldn't really draw any conclusions about it. The colour of the roses did worry her though. Thinking about the phone call, she rose from her desk and was gathering some notes and her mobile phone in preparation for the meeting upstairs when she looked up at the television set on her office wall. What she saw perplexed her even more. Reaching for the remote, she turned up the volume and watched the news stream showing a yacht's mast sticking out of the water with what appeared to be a wreath of black roses attached to it. A slight shudder ran up her spine. She picked up the desk phone and pressed the extension for the Chief Commissioner's Staff Officer.

"Anne Reid here, Inspector. Something very important has come up and I'll have to miss this morning's briefing." There was no argument from the Staff Officer who knew that the upstairs daily meeting was not missed through anything unimportant. Reid put the phone down for the second time, grabbed her mobile and rang Vince Anderson who she knew would be on his way in.

"Inspector Anderson, get in here as quick as you can, and on your way contact Tony Signorotto and get him and his people in here for a meeting. Something has happened and I have a feeling our fiend Bogdan Vulpe is behind it. While you're on your car phone get someone to pick up the wreath of black roses that was left at the yacht bombing in Brighton. If you have any problems getting it from the forensic people, tell them the pick-up has been authorised by the Deputy Commissioner Crime and it has connections to an international incident. All clear with that?"

"On the way, boss," a slightly bemused Anderson said as he parked his unmarked police car and called Tony Signorotto.

"Boss wants you, Kate and Max in her office within the hour. Something about Vulpe and a wreath of black roses. Don't ask me about it because I know as much as you do. She's obviously put two and two together about something and wants to see us all. I've got to go to the Royal Brighton Yacht Club and retrieve a wreath that was left at a bombing apparently."

"I've just seen the news about the yacht bomb and can possibly see what she's on about. The owner of the boat was just interviewed, and you wouldn't guess who it is," Signorotto said holding a piece of toast in one hand and the phone in the other as he ate a quick breakfast.

"Someone we know obviously," Anderson replied.

"His Honour Miles Wilson," Signorotto came back with.

"No wonder she's worried. See you soon at her office, Tony."

"I'll round up Kate and Max and be there as quick as I can."

***

By the time Max Tyler and Kate McLaren walked into the Superintendent's office, they could see Reid, Anderson and Signorotto standing over the centre table which was being covered by several large photos by Reid and at the other end adorned with a circular wreath made up entirely of black roses. The Superintendent indicated for all members to gather around the table before she spoke.

"You can all see this wreath. It was found at the scene of the bombing at the Royal Brighton Yacht Club last night," she said to all present. Heads nodded collectively. At the other end are several photos I have had my father in England send me. The photos show a similar wreath with black roses which was left at the doorstep of my parents' house in Surrey. The difference in the two is the one mysteriously left at their house is a note left with it. It read '*Best of health to Irene, Geoff and Anne.*' The boat that was targeted at the marina was named '*Legal Eagle*' and is owned by Justice Miles Wilson. I am drawing the obvious conclusion that Bogdan Vulpe is behind both the bombing and the house call, which I must say has shaken my dear parents no end."

"Boss, if it was Vulpe, how'd he get your parents address?" Tyler said.

Anne Reid tossed over a month-old copy of Police Life magazine to him. "When I got the job down here, I gave an interview to Police Life magazine. It's on page four and in it

I was asked about my life back in England. I mentioned my parents and the fact they lived in Cobham in Surrey. Wouldn't have been much to track them down after that."

"I've done some Googling on Justice Wilson and it turns out his yacht *Legal Eagle* was featured in the Herald Sun last summer when he entered it into one of the Round the Bay races. Quite a yachtsman, I'm told. Would have been easy to find out where his yacht was berthed," Tony Signorotto said.

"If Vulpe's idea of revenge is property damage and putting the frighteners on old people, then I think he might just be playing us," a furious Reid said to the others.

"Bring him in, boss?" a wide-eyed Max Tyler said eagerly.

"Absolutely," Reid said with steely determination. "He's behind this all right."

Chapter 21

Max Tyler led six members of the Critical Incident Response Team straight through the door and subsequent first floor of the Cleanstyle Industrial Cleaning Company. They weren't interested in anything on that floor even though Max was aware of the twenty-kilogram shipment of fentanyl that he knew was sitting somewhere nearby. If Bogdan Vulpe wanted to take this to a person level by intimidation methods, then Max was only too willing to oblige him. If Vulpe wanted personal, then that was what he was going to get. He led his team to the upstairs office, past some office workers who stood to one side when they saw the black clad members of the CIRT.

Bogdan Vulpe only had about one second to realise that someone had knocked on his office door before the brass handle flew from the inside and the door splintered down the middle and crashed to the floor revealing the black apparition of a CIRT member holding what was known in police circles as a 'twenty-pound key.' The heavy sledge hammer hung loosely in the right hand of the burly police officer. The 'key' had done its job. Vulpe stood, but before he could move, Max Tyler stepped through the doorway and held up a piece of blue paper.

"Sorry about the door, Bogdan, but I did call out three or four times for you to open it. Your hearing mustn't be too good," Max said smiling at the shocked looking Romanian behind the desk.

"What the fuck? Where do you or your black pyjama gang get the right for this?" an enraged Vulpe spat.

"From this little piece of paper here," Max said, holding up the search warrant before he slapped it on the desk in front of him. After discussions with Tony Signorotto and Vince Anderson they had applied for the warrant to search only in relation to Vulpe's office where they thought there might be some evidence connecting him to the yacht bombing and the delivery of the wreath in England. The last thing they wanted was anyone searching the building and finding the fentanyl. They knew that Anton Funan was downstairs and so to stop him from panicking, Tony and Kate McLaren had positioned themselves near him as he stood there gobsmacked. He knew nothing about this raid. Tony had already called out to anyone downstairs that this raid only concerned the first-floor office area. This turned Funan's look from one of panic to that of bewilderment. Meanwhile, Max continued with Vulpe.

"This is a warrant to search this office space in relation to the bombing of the yacht *'Legal Eagle'* at the Royal Brighton Yacht Club and..." Max was cut off mid-sentence by Vulpe.

"What the fuck has that got to do with me?" he said lying through his pearly white, perfectly formed teeth.

"This warrant also relates to the delivery of a package to the address contained within the warrant. It is an address in England," Tyler said.

"Again, you little public servant, what the fuck has that got to do with me?" Vulpe said a bit more quietly as his appreciation of how these members had pieced together the two wreaths so quickly had sunk in.

"A wreath of black roses was delivered to the premises of Geoff and Irene Reid in Surrey in England yesterday and there was a similar wreath found at the site of the yacht bombing at the Royal Brighton Yacht Club. The yacht belonged to a Supreme Court judge by the name of Miles Wilson. You were present in court some time ago when he sentenced one of your employees to prison for drug dealing. Connect that with the fact that the daughter of Geoff and Irene Reid happens to be the Superintendent that you spat at when you were arrested for threats to kill a witness involved in a case where you threatened her and I'd say we have justification for the search, don't you?" a smiling Max Tyler said.

"So what you loser. Search all you like. I know nothing about any of this, but I must say, these old people in England must have been scared. What a pity, eh?" Vulpe said breaking into a laugh. He knew that a search of his office would reveal nothing as he had disposed of the burner phones that he had contacted both Florin Barbu and his cousin Mercia Vulpe with. This was just a fishing exercise on behalf of the police. Vulpe didn't connect the dots though in relation to why they only wanted to search his office and nowhere else.

Max Tyler was going to take his time with the search, and he wasn't going to be too tidy about it. Vulpe sat down in an office chair with the left hand of a very serious looking CIRT member on his right shoulder. He hated being touched by any form of authority and he could not help but squirm in his seat.

"First things first, Bogdan. This warrant is also a seizure one, so the first thing you will hand over is your mobile phone, thanks. Then we will be taking, sorry, seizing every form of electronic hardware in this office. You will get them back but with our workload at the moment, don't hold your breath as to when that will happen."

Over an hour later and with the office area looking like a council tip, Max announced that they had finished, to which Vulpe attempted to knock the hand of the CIRT member from his shoulder, but all that achieved was a much harder grip.

"Get the fuck off me and get out. You've got nothing except for my phone and a couple of business laptops which will get you nowhere," the furious and sweating Romanian screamed.

"Oh, Bogdan, we might have finished here, but I have a verbal invitation for you, which Superintendent Reid totally agreed with," Tyler said as he removed his blue plastic gloves and dropped them in an office rubbish bin as he watched Vulpe's eyes widen at the disrespect of the act.

"It goes like this. *Bring him in!*"

Bogdan Vulpe was lifted physically from his chair, handcuffed for the second time by Max Tyler and dragged screaming from his office.

Two can play this game, Bogdan," Max said to Vulpe's reddened, vein popping face.

Chapter 22

Hours later, Anne Reid stepped into the interview room at Police Headquarters where Bogdan Vulpe sat with a smug look on his face. The English police officer was not about to mince her words as she stood over the top of the would-be gangster who had Max Tyler on one side of him and Vince Anderson on the other. Both police officers had questioned him extensively about the visit to Reid's parents' house in Cobham and the sinking of 'Legal Eagle' at the Royal Brighton Yacht Club. Even with playing the good cop, bad cop routine on him, neither member had got anything they could remotely use as evidence against him. They begrudgingly turned to their Superintendent. As she was about to speak, Vulpe got in first.

"Why don't we swap roles here, bitch. You spit at me and I'll wipe it off this time," the laughing Romanian said.

"If you think you're getting away with threatening my family, I'll come after you with everything at my disposal, Vulpe. You can sit here and deny it all you like, but we are onto you and your games."

"Don't know what you are talking about, but it is nice to have a bit of skirt doing the questioning for a change. Makes a change from the body odour of these two," he said looking first at Tyler then Anderson. "But I suppose they have had a hard time getting absolutely nowhere the last couple of hours. Now, I have places to go and people to see, darling, so I suggest you let me go right now before I have even more ammunition to give my lawyers to support my harassment claim against your fucking police department. You've dragged me down here after destroying my office, interrogated me about some shit regarding people from overseas and about some fucking yacht all because someone left some black roses lying around. I don't know how I've done anything to someone overseas seeing that I am here in Melbourne and secondly, I don't like boats and I've never been asked to be a member of this yacht club that you keep going on about. Your accusations are like all your others. Absolute crap," he said leering at Reid.

"Remember Vulpe, you are out on bail at the moment, and we have the right to bring you in for questioning regarding anything we believe you may have done in connection to committing crime. You and I know the yacht belongs to Judge Wilson, who happens to be the same judge that sent Cel Tradat down when he worked for you," Reid said in reply.

"Don't think he works for me, lady. I hear he had an accident in prison, but then again that's what happens to drug dealers, isn't it? They, like a lot of other people I know, end up dead. Now that we've met a couple of times, I put you into the category of people I know, so you'd better be careful. Don't be unlucky like Cel. That would be terrible, and I'd have to send a dozen roses to your funeral," Vulpe said breaking into an almost maniacal laugh before suddenly stopping and looking directly at Reid. "That would be a black day."

Vulpe never saw the slap coming. All he was left with was a loud buzzing in his ears, a very sore neck from having his head spun to one side so quickly and the thought that Reid slapped harder than some of his cohorts punched. He spat bloodied saliva onto the floor. Anderson and Tyler looked at Reid in disbelief.

"Your turn to spit again, eh, Bogdan?" Reid said with a look of satisfaction on her face. "If you are going to complain about something, I'd make it worthwhile. Just imagine if any of your contacts found out that you'd complained about being slapped by a little policewoman. You'd be the laughing stock of every bar in Fitzroy."

"You fucking bitch," Vulpe said standing from behind the interview table and starting to take a step around it, but not before receiving an even harder slap to the other side of his face, spinning him backwards. Vince Anderson immediately stepped between the two combatants.

"You want to threaten eighty-year-old people in their home then you can expect a lot worse than this you little prick," the diminutive English police officer said with venom in her voice. We are going to be all over you twenty-four seven you grubby little shite. You are scum. The fact that you hide behind some contact in England and can't even own up to what you did proves to me that you are rubbish. Now get out of here before I really work you over."

Vulpe didn't know how to react. He had never before been attacked verbally or physically by any female like this. His head was pounding and there was blood trickling down his chin from the second slap which had caused his nose to bleed.

"You'll pay for this. You will fucking pay for this. Wait till the Chief Commissioner sees the interview tape of this. You'll be charged with assault you little bitch," he said as Max Tyler shoved him out the door.

Vince Anderson didn't know what to say. He looked at the petite frame of his Superintendent and was gob smacked. Eventually, as Reid put her uniform jacket back on, he spoke.

"Ma'am, I'll turn the video off now?"

"No need. I turned it off just before I walked in, Detective Inspector. Seems to me, for all the talk I hear about you

Australians not putting up with bullshit, you and Detective Sergeant Tyler certainly listened to a lot of it from him."

"Not concerned about allegations, ma'am?"

Reid turned the door handle to leave and at the same time looked at her Detective Inspector.

"Vince, I have worked on train bombings, car bombings and every sort of terrorist situation you can think of back home. Bogdan Vulpe wouldn't be allowed to shine the shoes of people I've convicted. He's small fry, and there are two reasons I did what I did. I'm not the slightest bit concerned. First is that I did it on purpose to get him even madder at me and that has certainly happened, which will lead him to try and get revenge even quicker, and secondly, let him do his best with any complaint. By the time I must answer to the big bosses here, I'll be back sipping English breakfast tea with my folks. This is only a twelve-month secondment," she said with a wink as she departed the room. Anderson didn't move.

Don't like where this is headed. Like two boxers who are trying to land the killer blow!

Chapter 23

Anton Funan could see by the look on Vulpe's face that the reason he had been called into his boss's office was that he was not a happy man. He cautiously sat on the opposite side of the desk and waited for Vulpe to start speaking. Time passed slowly as he could feel sweat trickling down under his shirt. He knew he hadn't done anything to upset his boss but then again, he was also there when Vulpe was unceremoniously dragged from the building in handcuffs so his mood now would be very dark. Vulpe turned quickly and spoke in what seemed a relatively calm voice.

"Where are we at with that fentanyl? Who's the buyer?"

"At the moment we have an Asian cartel who wants it. I put it out to the contact list that you gave me, but no-one wants to touch it. It's all too new here for them. Right now, it's this Asian lot. They know who the bidding war is against, and they don't seemed fazed by the reputation of the Black Knights.

"What about the Black Knights? They would want it seeing it's come from one of theirs to begin with. They'll think it's their right to be the distributors. Have they contacted you?" Vulpe said.

Funan had been in contact with the undercover police officer that rode with the Black Knights, but he had been waiting for days for him to get back with a bid.

"Yeah, I'm waiting to see what they offer. It's been a few days, but they haven't got back to me yet," a nervous Funan replied.

"If you get a close enough offer for the shipment from them, do the deal. They'll know we have it here because the Romanian chapter shipped it here. I don't want to get involved with some Asian drug cartel just to save a few thousand dollars. Ring that bikie contact now and see what they offer. Put him on speaker," an insistent Vulpe said.

Funan punched in the number slowly and when it was answered he immediately gave the signal that there were other people involved in the call. He was told to use the phrase 'fen man,' if he wasn't alone

"It's fen man here. Need to find out what you are doing?"

The U/C member came back with the answer which Tyler and Signorotto were always going to give because there were other plans to get the fentanyl. It was just timing that had to be correct.

"We will buy. Need a week to get the cash," the police member said.

"You know the price that you have to beat?" Funan said.

Putting on a show of true bikie bravado, the U/C shot straight back.

"It came from brothers, and it will be sold to brothers. I will contact you. Do not sell to anyone else."

The undercover operative had been with the Black Knights for three years now, but he knew, as did his Departmental handlers that when the proposed raid went ahead within the week it would be his last contact with the group. His exit strategy had been planned well in advance. The Black Knights would know immediately that if there was a raid on Vulpe's factory, the information could only have come through a snitch. He would be a dead man walking, but he wasn't worried. He would be sliding back into the real detective world under his own name and back to living at his own address hopefully. The Knights were tough, but they were also dumb. The beard and long hair and the fake overseas accent he had used since being with them would be gone.

Funan finished the call. He knew Vulpe's premises would be raided, and his boss would be arrested and charged with the importation of the fentanyl. Hopefully then he could get himself and his family out from underneath this man once and for all. He just had to be ready.

"We will give them one week. They either buy or I'll sell to the Asians. I haven't paid Romania for their goods, so I want a high price from the Knights. At least a two hundred percent profit margin, you understand Anton?"

Anton Funan understood. From his meetings with Tyler and Signorotto he knew that as soon as he was 'arrested' at the raid, he, and his family would go straight into the Witness Protection program. The only time he would have to face Bogdan Vulpe again was as a witness against him in court. He had to rely on Signorotto and Tyler in regard to getting off the charges he was on.

Now it was a waiting game.

Vulpe dismissed him with a wave of his hand. He went back downstairs and continued to work with the legal cleaning contracts that they had.

Just try and act normal for the remaining time, he told himself.

Chapter 24

Bogdan Vulpe had other things to arrange beside getting the fentanyl sold. His world was the distribution of illegal drugs first and the running of a successful contract cleaning company second. The trouble was, that violence coursed through his blood. Violence and the rage of a Romanian madman. He knew he should just forget the insults he had been handed by that bitch of a Superintendent, but his ego and his hot-blooded temper would never allow him to let the matter go. No matter what, she would never insult him again and there was one way to ensure this. She had to pay the ultimate price. Once again, he reached for the phone. He wanted the services of someone who needed money and would do anything to get it. A source of his had been keeping tabs on the person he was about to ring. It was fortunate timing as he had just completed a long prison stretch.

***

Dinu Luca hated Australia. Hated it because he had just finished eight years in Australia's Supermax prison, the Goulburn Correctional Centre in New South Wales for a brutal assault on a shopkeeper where a robbery had turned bad not only for the victim but also for Luca because his accomplices had driven off and left him at the scene. The New South Wales Armed Robbery Squad had a reputation for getting their man and so it was for Luca. Prior to being sentenced to the lengthy prison term, he had been handed a severe lesson in why not to be apprehended by one of the most feared group of detectives in the land. His first year of imprisonment had consisted mainly of rehab in the prison hospital.

Luca was now in his mid-forties but his reputation as a standover merchant had only been enhanced with his time in Supermax. Luca ruled with fear and retribution inside. He had no family in Australia and believed the only way was to get back to Romania and pick up his bad habits again with a bit of luck and some low life connections. He was lying on a dirty mattress in a flop house in Paddington when the scruffy manager walked in.

"Call for you downstairs. Someone from Melbourne. Hurry up and take it," the lanky dirty-haired youth said to Luca without any show of respect as he turned his back on him.

Luca put a shirt on over his dirty singlet, grabbed a cigarette from the pack beside his single bed and walked down the stairs to the foyer of the run-down so-called guest house before picking up the grime covered receiver from the counter.

"Yes," was all he said.

"Dinu Luca, this is a call from a person who would like to offer you employment for one job here in Melbourne. It requires your expertise for bringing things to a conclusion. Are you interested?" Bogdan Vulpe said from a burner phone in his office.

"Who's this? How did you find me?" Luca said quickly.

"All can be discussed later. I am of Romanian birth, and I am in Melbourne. I know you are out, and I presume you would like to make money. I can offer you very good money if you bring a job to... *termination*. Are you interested?"

"What area would this job centre around?" Luca said knowing full well it would be a contract killing. He didn't care one iota who he had to dispose of as long as he could add a requirement to the hit. "I could be interested, but I need to know two things. The first is more of curiosity and the second is a non-negotiable requirement."

"What are they?" Vulpe said quietly. The money had not been mentioned so he knew he could control that.

"Who is it that I would be dealing with and the second is that as well as the money, the contract will require a one-way ticket home."

"The contract concerns a female that is working in state law enforcement. The second is guaranteed along with half the contract price prior to the fulfilling of the contract. Now, I'll only ask one more time. Are you interested?"

"Yes," came the reply immediately.

"Good. Go and get a burner phone today and call me tomorrow. I will give you the details. You will then fly to Melbourne where you will be picked up. I will re-imburse you for your flight when you get here. Understood?"

Luca tried to hide his excitement at the prospect of a contract and a return to his home.

"I'll buy one within the hour and be back here straight away," Luca said hanging up and heading for the door. As he did, the youth from behind the counter yelled out.

"Don't forget, you owe for the room upstairs. Tomorrow at the latest."

Luca felt the rolled-up bundle of notes from his prison savings that was in his pocket. He had no intention of paying the pimply-faced piece of shit behind the counter. In fact, he thought he might just give him a broken arm before he left tomorrow. Heading for the nearest street corner he looked to find himself a pusher who would sell him a burner phone. He could smell his homeland already.

Chapter 25

Yang Chen was not prepared to wait any longer while Anton Funan went back and forth between possible buyers for the fentanyl shipment. One of the contacts that Funan had been given by Bogdan Vulpe had said no to the prospect of buying but passed Chen's phone number to Funan as a possible interest.

Chen was certainly interested but wasn't going to haggle over price. He was the new breed of Chinese dealers who had broken away from the Triad elders. He wanted to do business quickly and Funan had made a big mistake by letting Chen know that the Black Knights were also in the mix. When pressed further, Chen was told that the winning bid was down to either him or the Black Knights. To Chen's way of thinking there was a simple answer and that was to eliminate the opposition. The Black Knights did not scare a man who had been brought up on Triad ways. Torture and execution did not faze him in the slightest. It was just a matter of eliminating the opposition and taking the drugs from Funan or whoever was his boss. The first was easy but the second was harder because he didn't know the location of the shipment.

Chen had never seen Funan before, so he called for a face-to-face meeting with him on neutral territory. The Chinese Lion restaurant in Little Bourke Street in the CBD was settled on. He didn't need a meeting to plead for the sale because he would never plead. What he wanted was to see Funan so when the meeting was concluded he could have him followed by one of his loyal underdogs.

The lunch had gone off well, with Chen insisting on paying for everything. The shipment and price were discussed in quiet tones as were more mundane things such as Funan's family life. Chen could not believe how naive Funan was. They parted on good terms with Funan indicating that he would get back in contact in a day or so and believed that Chen would get the shipment. Chen knew damn well that he would get it because he was taking it very soon.

Anton Funan had no idea that when he left the Cleanstyle Cleaning Company later that day he was being followed very discreetly by several Chinese tags all the way to his family home in Reservoir. While he settled in for the evening with his wife and child, he thought about the future without Bogdan Vulpe.

***

Driving out of his garage the next morning and heading to work after waving goodbye to his wife as she loaded their son into the car for the daily transport to the nearby St Gabriel's Primary School, he took no notice of the Toyota Supra that overtook him in The Broadway and suddenly stopped in front of his car. Funan looked quickly in the rear-view mirror only to see a dark coloured Ford Transit van come to a halt just inches behind him. Two Asian males immediately jumped out of the van and walked quickly to his driver's window.

Funan didn't like guns, but he immediately reached into the glovebox and attempted to get the small Beretta pistol that was located there. Before he could, he heard and felt the drivers' window being smashed in before an electric shock ran through his body and he slumped over the steering wheel with his mind descending into a fog.

It was all over in less than a minute. The Chinese hijackers had done their job. While they manhandled

Funan's limp body from his car and into the Transit van, they had already stopped any vehicle from approaching them from behind because they had placed two fake Hi-Vis clad traffic workers back down The Boulevard to direct any rear approaching cars into a side street for the short amount of time their compatriots needed to get Funan loaded. Within two minutes, the lead car, Transit van, Funan's car and the traffic workers had disappeared, leaving several confused drivers to meander the side streets of Reservoir looking for the usual directional signs that would get them back onto The Boulevard. When they did re-appear onto their original route, they all felt they had returned to their normal mundane routine. Happiness was the same old route to work. They had seen nothing.

In the meantime, the Chinese convoy had travelled slowly to Chen's headquarters in Carlton where, behind a quickly shut roller door, Funan was unceremoniously dumped onto the concrete garage floor. When he slowly came around, he could still feel the electric tingle of the stun gun that had been activated on his neck before it had sent him into unconsciousness. He was suddenly dragged up onto a wooden chair, hands and wrists bound to it. Shaking his head in a futile attempt to get rid of the severe headache the stun gun had given him, he looked at the blurry but recognisable face of Yang Chen. With a very dry mouth he attempted to speak.

"Why? Why?" was the only word he could utter.

"Because, Anton, I've decided just to take that shipment of fentanyl. That's why," the sadistically smiling face of Chen said.

"But in a few days' time it would be yours."

"We are taking it tonight, you fool, and we aren't paying for it. Now I want to know where it is stored. I will not play games with you. You will be given only one chance."

A completely confused Funan looked up at Chen who was now holding a pistol by his side. "What do you think you're doing, Chen? I'm only the middle man. The fentanyl isn't mine. I'm just negotiating on behalf of the main guy. I have no say in anything except the price he wants," he said with a now panicking rise in his voice.

Chen smiled as he pressed the barrel of the pistol to Funan's forehead.

"The one thing you do know is the location of the shipment, is that correct?"

A sweating Anton Funan nodded his head in reply.

"That's what I want to know. You will now tell me where it is and tonight, we will take you there. You show us where it is, we take it, and you save your miserable life. Sounds like a deal I would take, eh?"

Even Anton Funan, who wasn't the smartest person on the drug scene knew that he had about twenty-four hours maximum left in his miserable life. The only thing to do was to give Chen the information he wanted. Either way, he knew he was a dead man walking. If he didn't hand over the information, he would be a dead man crawling once these Chinese goons had finished going over him. He proceeded to tell Chen the details of Vulpe's warehouse together with information regarding the alarm system and the exact location of the fentanyl.

"You are going to help us tonight, Anton, and then you will be set free," a straight-faced Chen said without any emotion in his voice.

Now that I know who you are, I don't think so, Funan thought desperately.

Chapter 26

Anton Funan went through the motions punching in the code numbers to unlock the safety padlock at the side of the Cleanstyle Industrial Company building. He had no idea what time it was. All he knew was that it was late, and it was dark. He just wanted the night to be over one way or the other.

As the alarm light went to green giving safe entrance to the building, he opened the small steel door that was located within the big front roller door and stepped into the cavern-like darkness of the building followed by Chen and two of his associates.

"There is no-one in here besides us?" Chen queried Funan.

"No-one. It's just us," Funan replied thinking that the stars that he had seen in the sky outside were the last he was going to see. It was too late to regret a life that had been embedded so much in crime. You live by the sword, you ultimately die by the sword, or in this case probably by a Chinese manufactured pistol.

Funan had already told Chen that the fentanyl was packed inside a crate marked *Industrial Cleaning Machinery* and that it was down towards the rear of the factory. Chen had left a third goon behind and Funan could now hear a vehicle being backed down through the internal path of the factory. Seconds later a Chinese Great Wall utility slowly pulled up near them.

"Walk us to the crate," Chen said quickly at the same time as shoving Funan sharply in the back, causing the scared Romanian to fall over. Funan could see sweat all over Chen's face as though he was extremely hot.

It's cold in here. This guy's on something, Funan thought with trepidation as he walked in the torchlight over to the large wooden crate containing the drugs and pointed towards it. As he turned around to face Chen, he saw the eyes of the madman. The pupils were like pinpoints. As he lowered his gaze, he immediately noticed Chen screwing a silencer onto the end of the pistol he was holding.

"You will help load the box onto the back of this utility," Chen said in-between rapid breaths.

"You'll need the forklift from over there," Funan said indicating a yellow Toyota forklift parked nearby. "I can operate it and lift the crate."

"Do it," Chen said hurriedly, waving his pistol not only at Funan but at his accomplices also.

Funan knew his quickly devised plan had little or no chance of working but he was determined to take at least one of his abductors with him before he stepped off into the black void. He walked over to the forklift and stepped up into the driver's seat before switching the ignition key on and starting the big machine. He reversed the Toyota and swung the two protruding metal forks to a position just under the drug crate before manoeuvring them into the correct position in the pallet that the crate sat on and slowly raised it up to a height near the back of the utility's bed. He thought of his son and his wife as he looked down at Chen and his men who were all holding pistols by their sides. Beckoning one of the men to a position between the front of the crate and the forks, he closed his eyes and gunned the forklift forward, accelerating it straight at his now shocked target.

All bodies bar one jumped out of the way as the fork-lift rammed into the crate. The goon that had the shocked look on his face now wore it permanently. The only thing that added to his shock was looking down at one of the forks that had entered his now shaking body just below his rib cage. It had proceeded through him, snapping his spine and continuing through, pinning him to the crate full of fentanyl.

Funan jumped quickly off the seat and raced to the now dead, but still jerking mannequin and made a grab for his gun. Anton Funan was never going to be given the chance to reflect on his actions as he lifted the heavy calibre, blood covered pistol and began to swing it around in an arc towards anyone that was in range. The foolish action was never going to succeed.

The scream that he heard was his own, as the shots fired by Chen's automatic slammed into his body and stitched him from head to toe. Hitting the ground at the feet of the dead 'forked' Chinese, he looked up only to see Chen standing over him. An empty pistol magazine hit him in the head as he saw Chen slam a new fifteen round mag into his pistol and slide the top of the gun back with a resounding clacking sound. Funan knew he had only seconds to live so he closed his eyes and tried to think of his family. The picture turned from beautiful to black as the sound and then the feeling of a shot echoed through his now splattered brain. The stars he saw in his final moment were not those of the night sky outside.

Chen ordered his remaining men to pull their fellow countryman off the fork and drag him to the van. He then got them to do the same with Funan's body. Once dumped inside, they went to work albeit without the help of the blood covered fork lift and lifted, pushed and shoved the machinery crate into the back of the van. When that was complete, they all got into the vehicle and drove slowly to the front roller door. Chen did not care about Funan. He was going to die moments after he had helped them load the crate. The only down side was that he had wasted a lot more ammunition on him than he would have normally, but then again, Chen's anger had been raised by Funan's foolish actions.

Chen and his crew exited the factory and headed to a Chinese owned pig farm on the western outskirts of the city where the swine were going to receive some extra unexpected rations in an hour or so. There would be no questions asked by the farmer, who was an associate of Chen. The quicker he could fatten his pigs, the quicker they were slaughtered and the quicker the dim sim market received their supplies.

Chapter 27

Bogdan Vulpe stared at the empty space where the crate of fentanyl laden machinery had been on the factory floor. He raised his eyes to the blood smeared fork lift and the blood stains on the concrete. He had already rung Anton Funan to no avail. He cursed himself for not having fixed the security camera at the front door which the police had *accidently* broken in their latest raid on his premises. The phone call from Codrin Dalca had already come back in the negative. Funan had not picked up his son from school and had not been home all night. He saw no reason for believing Funan would double cross him because his family was at stake. No, he had to go along with the thought that Funan had been taken or disposed of in the theft of the fentanyl.

This was shaping as a disaster. He hadn't paid his overseas Romanian contact for the fentanyl and was treading a fine line financially until it was to have been on-sold to the Black Knights here. He now wished he hadn't given them an extra week to buy it. He had also made a verbal promise to pay Luca for a hit on his nemesis, Superintendent Anne Reid. He couldn't go back on that, or he'd lose face with any fellow mafioso.

His crazed mind could only think of one solution to what were in truth, two entirely different scenarios. He couldn't report anything to the police, even the possible abduction or murder of Anton Funan. Turning quickly and walking to his office, he shouted out to Codrin Dalca. "My office now!"

Dalca started towards the upstairs office, all the time thinking that his boss would want some hints on who would have dared raid the factory. He had no idea whatsoever. He was just a foot soldier, not a lieutenant like Funan was. After all, Vulpe had put Funan in charge of everything to do with the fentanyl. Dalca closed about the office door behind him and turned to see an enraged look on Vulpe's face as he sat behind his desk thumping his right fist on top of a sheath of papers.

"If they think she can do this to me, they are dead!" Vulpe screamed at the top of his voice.

A now frightened Codrin Dalca looked at his boss and without thinking replied.

"Who are you talking about boss?"

Vulpe screamed at his employee and at the same time launched a large and heavy cut glass ashtray over his head, causing it to crash loudly against the wooden door frame.

"Who do you fucking think, you idiot. That bitch Reid and her boys, Signorotto, Tyler and anyone else that has anything to do with us since Cel Tradat was sent down. That prick of a judge is probably bankrolling this heist for them. They are going to pay and pay in a big way. That bitch has done this as revenge for fucking with her family back home. It's time to show that pommy bitch who runs this state."

"What make you think it's the cops? How would they know about the fentanyl? They would have raided us weeks ago when we first got the shipment," an amazed Dalca said back to his boss. If the word got out that the cops were dealing in fentanyl, everyone would soon know. Can't see it, boss. This must be someone that Anton had been dealing with and wasn't happy about the wait or the price. Has to be."

Bogdan Vulpe stopped pacing about his office and stared at Dalca. He knew in the back of his mind that his employee was probably correct, but he was so enraged about the police and the judicial system that he had to blame them and take revenge, no matter what the cost.

"You start looking into who Anton was dealing with. The Black Knights were waiting another week to see about the buy. Just approach them straight up. If it was only them though, there wouldn't have been any bidding war that Anton mentioned. There must be something else in this. I still say the cops and that English bitch are involved. They couldn't get me any other way, so they want to send me broke. I reckon they have found some third party that owes them a favour to do me over. Drop everything else you're doing. Hand over the cleaning stuff to someone on our legit side and the day to day heroin stuff to someone you trust within the organisation. I want answers. I have a big contract to pay for and I want that fentanyl back."

Codrin Dalca could see Vulpe's mind turning over quickly, and he didn't like what he saw or what he could sense with his boss's dark mood.

"You're the boss. What are you going to do?"

"I've got someone else coming in to do some contract work for me, so I'll be busy with other things. I have to pay him big money so the quicker the fentanyl comes back, or you persuade whoever took it to cash up for it, the quicker I can pay this guy. His name's Dinu Luca and he's just got out of gaol in New South Wales. He'll be arriving here tonight."

"Dinu Luca? From what I have heard about him and his reputation, boss, he's nothing but a hired gun. He won't help you with any problems here. He's just a heavy for hire," Dalca said.

"He'll only be helping me eliminate some of our sideshow attractions so I can make the firm bigger," a now smiling Vulpe replied. "You just concentrate on who stole my shipment of fentanyl and get it back. Tell the world that Dinu Luca is now working for me. That should loosen a few tongues."

A now hesitant Codrin Dalca looked at his boss and spoke quietly. "Boss, please don't tell me that the sideshow attractions are in blue uniforms?"

"You didn't ask, and I didn't tell you. Leave the legal side of things to me. Well, me and Luca."

A shiver ran down Codrin Dalca's spine.

Chapter 28

Codrin Dalca knew he was taking a big risk standing outside the fortified gate of the Black Knights' clubhouse in Port Melbourne at midnight. There had been no word on the street after five days about the fentanyl heist. He had no choice in trying to keep Vulpe up to speed in his search but to do what he was about to do, and that was to approach Anton Funan's contact within the outlaw motor cycle gang.

He knew he was being watched on CCTV as he could see the cameras in the yard facing him. After waving his arms around to deliberately attract the attention of the night guard member, he heard, then saw the huge steel gate which was adorned by a massive painting of a black knight astride a Harley Davidson start to creak and slide sideways just enough to allow him to step inside. There was no going back at this point. Two steps into the well-lit yard and he felt the steel of a double barrel shotgun in his back. He immediately raised both his hands as a voice boomed over a loud speaker that was attached to the front of the steel reinforced clubhouse.

"Stay with your hands in the air while the boys search you. If you have a shooter on you, it would be wise to say so now. If they find one, it will be used to blow a hole through your knee. We will give you a choice as to what knee though," the voice said breaking into a maniacal laugh.

Dalca shook his head from side to side and called out. "No shooter, no weapons. I just want to talk to someone." There was silence as two large pairs of hands searched him from top to toe. When they were done, he was pushed into a kneeling position surrounded by three bikies, all wearing their club colours on their leather jackets. One still had the short-barrelled shotgun trained on him. The voice came again through the loud speaker.

"What do you want? We don't do visitors here. You only get in here if you're invited."

"My name is Dalca, Codrin Dalca and I work for Bogdan Vulpe. I need to talk to whoever it is that was dealing with our associate, Anton Funan."

The mention of Vulpe's name must have struck a chord with whoever was behind the loud speaker. Dalca could feel the end of the shotgun barrel being moved away from the top of his spine. Quiet words were being exchanged between the three bikies that had him pinned on the ground. Seconds passed before the voice came back over the yard.

"We want to know why you are here and not Funan."

Dalca was now going to take the biggest risk of the night.

"Because he's dead, or at least kidnapped."

"What's that got to do with the Black Knights?" the disembodied voice said flatly.

"Because not only is he dead or missing, but the fentanyl has been hijacked from our warehouse. The deal he was talking to one of you about is fucked. Vulpe knows there were others who wanted the shipment, so we need to find out who. We are going after them."

"How do you know we don't have it?"

"There's no word on the street about the shipment and I reckon two things. First is that you would have already started to move the gear which would have caused a lot of talk out there with other street level dealers like yourselves and secondly is that I wouldn't have got this far with you talking about it. You would have knocked me up as soon as I mentioned it."

A full minute or two went by before the voice spoke again, but this time it wasn't to him.

"Bring him inside. The Sergeant-at-Arms wants to speak to him."

With that, Dalca was lifted up and roughly shoved towards a door that had just been opened in the wall of steel in front of him. Once inside he was unceremoniously pushed down onto a wooden chair that was on one side of an old kitchen table. On the other side sat a large leather clad bikie.

"I'm the Sergeant-at-Arms of the Black Knights. I was arranging a deal with him for us, and I was going to get back to him any day now. What the fuck has happened to him and more importantly, what the fuck has happened to the fentanyl? We were the first-choice buyers."

"Five days ago, there was a raid on our factory in Collingwood in the early hours. The crate of machinery which had the fentanyl was taken and there was blood all over the floor. The CCTV cameras had been destroyed in a police raid, so we don't know who it was. Funan hasn't been found so we are presuming he is shark food in the bay or something now. His missus and kid haven't seen him, and if you knew Funan, his family is the biggest thing in his life, or it's starting to look like it *was* his biggest thing."

The Sergeant-at-Arms, Pete English, stared back at Dalca for a long while before speaking.

"Who else knew about the shipment?" he said knowing full well that the only other organisation that was trying to get their hands on it was a Chinese syndicate. Funan had never given him details of it other than to say that they were a new player on the scene.

"There is a Chinese connection, but Funan never told us who it was. We knew it was you and them, that's all. The fentanyl came from your lot in Romania, but we have never dealt with any Asians before. We are going to get it back from whoever it was that raided us."

"Well, we had the money ready, but the deal obviously never happened. No skin off our noses. You're on your own with a guess about the Chinese, but if you are going to mess with the old Triad in Little Bourke Street, be prepared for a fight to the death. They won't give it up," the Sergeant-at-Arms said indicating to his offsiders to escort Dalca back outside the premises. The bikie had more pressing matters to deal with now he had been told this news.

"You've got no idea who this Chinese crew could be?" Dalca said hopefully as a set of meaty hands picked him up.

"No fucking idea whatsoever," the bikie lied.

Dalca was dumped back outside on the footpath without further ado.

Ten minutes later, after the other bikies went back to their booze and cards, the Sergeant-at-Arms wandered away to the back of the yard and made a call to one of his counterparts at the Victoria Police Asian gang squad. Like himself, all undercovers knew nothing but a twenty-four-hour clock. It was picked up immediately.

"Hey, Chi, how the fuck are you? Still making those dim sims down at the South Melbourne market? Listen, I need to meet up with you and some members quickly. Can you do a meet tomorrow? Thanks mate. I'll get back to you as soon as I can. This is a big one." The next phone call was to Tony Signorotto.

"Tony, Pete English here," the undercover member whose true identity was Detective Leading Senior Constable Rick Waters said. "Lock it in, meeting tomorrow with you and your lot and Chi Quang from the Asian squad.

The old Carlton cop shop at ten. No uniforms."

Tony Signorotto, who had woken out of a deep sleep next to his wife Susie said, "We'll be there," as he collapsed back on his pillow.

Romanians, bikies and now Asians. I'm getting too old for this shit.

Chapter 29

Even though he was outranked by everyone at the meeting, there was no doubt in everyone's mind as to who was running it: Leading Senior Constable Rick Waters, the erstwhile Pete English, Sergeant-at-Arms of the Black Knights Outlaw Motor Cycle Gang.

The meeting was arranged for six in the morning to try to prevent any prying eyes wondering why several men and women were entering by the locked side door of the old but yet to be sold Carlton Police station in Drummond Street, Carlton. The only key to the premises was with Tony Signorotto at the new station. From time to time a real estate agent arranged by the State Government would get it from him to show a potential buyer through the historic and classified building. There had been no offers made on it once the historic overlays on the site were explained to potential customers. They all wanted to make money, not overspend on an unknown something in a fragile economy. It had proved to be a bonus from time to time for different police meetings such as this one.

Standing and seated inside the old watch-house were Anne Reid, Vince Anderson, Tony Signorotto, Kate McLaren, Max Tyler and Chloe Schaeffer. Also in the room were Rick Waters and Detective Senior Constable Chi Quang from the Asian Squad. Rick Waters started the ball rolling.

"Thanks for coming everyone. Don't normally go out of my adopted character, so to help me stay true to my 'colours', excuse the pun, could you just call me by my street name which is Pete." Nods from all around the room agreed with him.

"Last night at the rooms, we had a visit from a person looking for my help, which is most unusual seeing that my brothers only deal with helping themselves, not others. The visitor in question was Codrin Dalca who as we know works for Bogdan Vulpe.The reason for him making a late-night visit was to ask me, as the Knight's contact with Vulpe's organisation, if we had heard anything about their stolen shipment of fentanyl hitting the streets." This time, the faces just stared at him. Silence ensued.

Anne Reid cut to the chase very quickly.

"Pete, what the hell has happened?"

"Well, it's a fact that only the Knights and some Asian organisation have been looking seriously at the fentanyl that we know is, or was, stored in the Cleanstyle factory in Collingwood. That's a given. I was holding off on making the purchase for the Knights to give us all a better chance of conducting a serious raid and possibly catching Vulpe handing over the drugs to either the Knights or this other organisation that Anton Funan had told me about. Some Asian syndicate."

"If it had come down to the Black Knights making the buy, it would have been a raid where I would have had to come out from undercover and help with the arrests. I would then disappear from sight, and I was quite okay with that. I have been with them for a few years now and in actual fact probably six months too long. I was looking forward to a shower, haircut and shave," the long greasy-haired Pete said with a laugh. "Turns out that five nights ago, I would say that a young version of the Little Bourke Street Triads have hit them and knocked off the goods." Stopping to let this sink in with the crew around him, Pete indicated to Chi for him to take over.

"Folks, my name is Chi Quang, and I am with the Asian

Squad. We have been listening for some time now about a young, heavy and impatient crew led by a vicious individual by the name of Yang Chen. He has upset the old Triad members by wanting to take over all drug related operations in Melbourne. The older men did not want to know about this fentanyl shipment we have been informed. Pete knows by dealing with Anton Funan that only two groups were down for the buy. His Knights and an unknown Chinese group. I can tell you that it isn't anyone of the traditional Chinese crime gangs, so I am guessing that it is this breakaway mob that have jumped the gun before Vulpe's man decided on the buyer. So, what I'm saying is that while you have your problems reeling in Bogdan Vulpe, he is now looking for whoever stole his fentanyl. I'll pass back to Pete now for some more bad news."

The members were individually trying to take in what this meant to their job of stopping Vulpe when Pete started up again.

"Tony? Vince? Has anybody had contact with Anton Funan in the last five days?"

"He was due to get back to us when the shipment was due for sale, so in answer to your question, no we haven't. Is this the bad news on top of the bad news bit, Pete?" Tony Signorotto said.

"Well, whoever snatched the shipment also either snatched or dispatched Funan. Dalca said there was blood over the floor where the crate containing the fentanyl was. He hasn't been seen anywhere including home. Funan's wife hasn't reported him missing or anything. At least that is what I read between the lines from what Dalca said."

"Okay then," Reid stood up and spoke." We have a situation where we were trying to get Vulpe by waiting till he sold the shipment and now we look as though we have lost our one contact with his organisation. This is not good people. We can't let that fentanyl out on the street, so we have to go with the theory that this young Asian has lifted it. Do you have any idea as to who this new Chinese mob are, Detective Quang?"

"Yes and no, ma'am. We usually get nothing but silence from the Triads but one of our team has a girlfriend whose grandfather is connected in that area. She told our man that her grandfather was physically threatened just a few weeks ago if there wasn't a move by the Little Burke Street Triad to start handing over the reins of their operation to a new, and as her grandfather put it, '*a new generation of younger men.*' I am getting the whole team onto this today because not only do we need to stop the fentanyl from hitting the streets, but we are also looking at abduction or murder seeing that this Anton Funan has disappeared."

"Vince, Tony, anyone, is there any point in bringing Vulpe back in for questioning?" Reid said.

"No, not really," Tony Signorotto said. "He won't tell us anything. He's lost a shipment of drugs which he has probably paid for, so I think he'll be doing the same as us and that is going after the ones that did the heist. You agree people?"

"Tony's right, ma'am," Vince Anderson said. We keep a close eye on him and who he talks to and sees. He will be desperate. We need to remember though; he is a loose cannon. We can't lose sight of the fact that he also has real hatred towards us. I think if we let Quang get stuck into his end and in the meantime, we dog Vulpe full time and see what cracks. Everyone agree?"

The members in the room all nodded their heads in agreement.

"Right, from now on till we fix this, everyone is in plain clothes. Tony, can you arrange rostering twenty-four seven?" Reid said.

"Will do ma'am. Max, you grab a member from Carlton that's on this afternoon. Use one of the plain cars from Carlton. Kate, have a look at the Carlton roster and pick out a few for the next few days. One of us will have to be with whoever it is you pick. Okay people let's get this sorted. I don't like drugs anytime, but this sort of stuff combined with a possible new gang threat and a murder is not something I want happening, especially in or near my patch."

Chapter 30

Tony Signorotto always believed in leading his troops from the front and this was no exception. He decided to take it upon himself to fill the void alongside Max Tyler. As he sat back in the unmarked police sedan down the road from the factory, he quietly smiled to himself before he spoke to his junior Sergeant.

"I'd reckon you'd rather be sitting next to your girlfriend than some grumpy old Senior Sergeant who snores, eh Max?"

"You go to sleep on me, and you'll get an elbow in the ribs, Senior Sergeant or not," a smiling Max Tyler said to his old mentor as he adjusted the lens on the powerful Leica camera he had set up on the dashboard facing the front roller door of Vulpe's business. They had been sitting in the car for over three hours now and the sun was just starting to set. No-one except Vulpe and Codrin Dalca had entered the premises. They hadn't been there for the factory start time, but they presumed that the employees that were coming and going by Cleanstyle vans were just workers.

"It's funny you know," Signorotto said. "If all the vans that have come and gone are all doing legit business for Cleanstyle, then I can't fathom why Vulpe doesn't stick to making big bucks from his cleaning company. Why put yourself out there as Romanian mafioso and risk everything?"

"I think you hit the nail on the head when you said the word Romanian. It's where he thinks he should be in the world. I reckon he spends half the day and night brooding over why his Italian counterparts don't have anything to do with him. Inferiority complex is what it is," Max said siting still as he looked through the lens finder. "Hold on. Some head is getting out of a taxi outside the factory. Got to get some shots of him. Salty looking dude as Clint Eastwood would say," Max said as he set the camera to automatic setting off a series of quick clicking sounds as it recorded the man's movement from paying for the taxi until he walked through the factory door. In the meantime, Signorotto had been eyeing the man through a large set of field glasses. Something didn't bode well with him.

"Get some of those over now to the techs and the team. I want to know who that is. He walks as though he owns the place. Gives me an uneasy feeling, that bloke," Signorotto said icily.

Max attached a small device to the side of the camera and downloaded the pictures onto his phone. Minutes later they were on their way in email form.

"Kate will get the facial recognition people onto this asap," Signorotto said as he phoned his fellow Senior Sergeant.

"Sorry, Kate," he said as she picked up the call." I know you are probably getting ready to come down here and take over, but Max just sent you an email with some pics of some dude that just went into our premises. Doesn't matter if you are late down here, I want to know who this fella is. He just gives off bad vibes if you know what I mean."

"No problem Tony, I'll get onto the experts right now. Local do you think?"

"Maybe but try interstate as well. He didn't bring a car. He came by taxi and paid in cash. We have the number of the taxi, so I'll send that in also. You'll need to get onto Yellow Cabs and find out where the fare was picked up. He looked European and I'm thinking Romanian. If that's so, we have a new player in the game beside Vulpe and Dalca. I'm starting to think we need to keep an eye on our judge also in the short term, but I'll speak to Reid and Anderson later about that. At the moment, if this guy has anything to do with Vulpe then right now we have those two and Dalca in the same building which I suppose is a bonus. Anyway, I'll let you get on with it. See you when we see you."

After Signorotto sent the taxi number to Kate, there was nothing to do but wait.

***

The big figure of Dinu Luca stepped into Vulpe's office without any knock on the door. Codrin Dalca stood up as he entered but stepped back as the rough looking individual passed him without even looking and sat down on the other side of the desk to Vulpe.

"You've got me here, so let's get on with it. Who's the hit on?" Luca said in a low business-like voice. Codrin Dalca went cold. He knew Vulpe was more concerned with revenge at this point in time rather than trying to find out who had his fentanyl shipment. Dalca wanted nothing to do with any type of hit on anyone, especially anyone in law enforcement. Vulpe had told him only that night that Luca would be arriving and to sort him out some weaponry. Dalca took a chance.

"Boss, how about we concentrate on the fentanyl before this?"

"We can do both. How are you getting on with finding it?" Vulpe said in a derogatory tone in reply.

"You said no-one else knew it was here beside the Black Knights and this Chinese mob. Well, I told you I've spoken to the Knights and I'm convinced they didn't do it, so I've got some people sniffing around Little Bourke Street and the Triads. A name will come up for sure. There's no word on the streets yet so it hasn't been sourced out yet."

Luca looked from Dalca to Vulpe. "Something else I can help with? For a price of course," Luca said with a straight face.

"I don't care if you have to walk into every fucking Dumpling King or Chinese massage parlour between here and fucking Mildura, Dalca. Get it sorted. I want my happy ending, and I'm not talking about at the hands of some skinny little broad covered in massage oil. I'm starting to get pretty pissed off with your efforts in this." With eyes looking from Dalca to Luca and back again, Vulpe lent forward on his elbows and spoke quietly.

"I may have other people who want a permanent job here, now, so I suggest you get off your skinny arse and get me my fentanyl back. Fuck off for now," Vulpe said loudly as he waved Dalca to the door. Watching the gobsmacked employee depart the room, he turned his attention to Luca.

"I'm doubling the price. There's two I want knocked. One bitch copper and one fucking judge. Can you handle both?"

Dinu Luca looked at Bogdan Vulpe for about three seconds before he spoke.

"The Pope a fucking Catholic? Of course I can handle both. For the right price!"

"Of course, of course," Vulpe said thinking that he'd just about have to sell the factory to pay for the hits. The vortex that he was entering with taking on the state's justice system never crossed his one-track mind.

Chapter 31

It was after midnight by the time Kate McLaren and her partner got to the stake-out with the information that Tony wanted. They slipped quietly into the rear seat of the unmarked police car and were immediately enveloped in a fog of body odour.

"Geez, you two could do with a dab of deodorant. Smells like a football changeroom in here," Kate said.

Without missing a beat, Max Tyler chipped in. "Trust you to be hanging around football changerooms, Kate," he said pressing the button to let one of the windows down as Kate clipped him across the back of his head in a friendly manner.

"What info have you got, Kate?" Tony Signorotto said with a tired sounding voice.

"Well, it didn't take the techs and the facial recognition guys long. The individual's name is one Dinu Luca. Released from Goulburn in New South Wales after serving eight years for a botched armed rob and assault. Has reputation as a Romanian heavy and gun-for-hire according to the boys in Sydney. While he was inside, he put numerous others in the prison sick bay for minor things. There are a couple that will never walk without a limp again. Shoved a plastic fork though one guy's eye just because he didn't say excuse me when he reached in front of Luca to pick up a sauce bottle. Our brothers up north reckon that he could have got out in four, but he kept the bad attitude going so they kept adding time to his sentence."

"What did the taxi firm give us?" Max said.

"Was picked up from Tullamarine after a flight from Sydney earlier today and brought straight here. No luggage or anything about hotels or such. The driver said he didn't say a word until he got here. Paid with a one hundred dollar note and didn't even ask for change."

"If I know my crooks and their habits, then this guy is here for a job, and I don't mean working in the cleaning business. Vulpe has hired this guy for a reason. I don't think it will be anything to do with the missing fentanyl if he's down from Sydney and just out of the can. He won't know the scene here or any of the players. I'd lay good money that Vulpe is about to up the ante on some sort of payback to us. He's as guilty as hell for the boat bombing and the threats to Reid's family back home. He didn't do it himself. He would have hired some Romanian explosives guy for that, and we know he has family back in England which I'll bet he used for the intimidation bit on Reid's parents," Signorotto said quietly.

"So if Vulpe isn't using him for finding his drugs, then what for?" Max chipped in.

"I think Superintendent Reid has gone a bit too far with our friend Bogdan," Tony said seriously. "She's okay at her job all right, but I don't think she has had any dealings with the Romanian mafioso before. Anderson said she has embarrassed Vulpe twice now and if I know anything about these pricks it is this: They'll want their revenge quick smart. I've rung Vince Anderson and he's putting round the clock surveillance and protection on Judge Wilson immediately. Chloe is driving for Reid, and they will have a Force Response guy with them but not for a couple of days. All their troops are committed to other jobs at the moment. In the meantime, Kate, you can have this lovely comfortable seat here till we get back in the morning. If you guys think that I need to be called, just call. This situation is going to come to a head quicker than we all think, I reckon," Tony said swapping car keys with Kate's young partner at the same time as indicating that he wanted to speak to her outside the car.

"Who's the young guy? One of ours?" Tony said looking through the window without trying to stare at the nervous looking police officer.

"Yeah, one of the newbies. Fresh out of the Academy. We're too short staffed so I thought he could get in a shift doing this while some of the regulars cover the cars and such," Kate said as she turned to the car.

"He looks about nineteen or twenty," Tony said.

"Spot on, boss. He's just turned twenty."

As Signorotto walked towards the other car, he couldn't help thinking that he really should start looking at his own future. His daughter Gracie was at school now and his wife Susie was back full time as manager of one of the Bank Vic branches. He knew that Susie wasn't happy about him being out on the streets again after all he had put into 'The Job' over the years and in his own mind he knew she was right. Members like Kate McLaren and Max Tyler were more than capable of running the show and he had found that he was worrying far too much about different jobs and cases these days. A recent coffee with his old Superintendent, now retired, Phil Stone, made him realise there was more to life than being a cop. Stone had picked up a job in customer service at the Melbourne Cricket Ground and was dabbling in a bit of writing. Stone didn't need the money, he just wanted different connections. Some of his former colleagues would forever be his friends but had told Signorotto that *'one day you'll wake up and know it's time to change buses.'*

Although Anne Reid was a thoroughly good officer, underneath it, Tony didn't like taking orders from someone who had been policing in London for her career. Carlton was not London and London crooks were not Carlton crooks. He was beginning to think she was only out for the biggest prize headline. In this instance it would be the fentanyl.

Tony didn't necessarily want to give up work, he just had the feeling that although his heart was still in it to a certain extent, he wasn't giving it the one hundred per cent concentration that it needed most of the time. His long-time friend, Dom Santino, the well-known owner of the famous Italian family restaurant in Lygon Street which went by the name '*Dom's*,' had approached him a few months before about coming into the business with him. Tony had laughed it off at first but the thought about still working in Carlton but not in the Police Force was starting to look like more appealing as time went by. He had mentioned it to Susie, and she was very enthusiastic about it. '*This is a game for the younger members now*' she had said.

Max Tyler drove back to the station in silence. He had been mentored by and worked with Tony for some years now and knew when to talk and when to shut up. This was a time to keep quiet. Tony was deep in thought and Max got the feeling that it wasn't about work. If it had been, Tony would have been throwing up ideas about the case to him, and he wasn't.

Chapter 32

Bogdan Vulpe had no idea that while he was inside his cleaning business he was being watched by the police. He had his mind set on two things. The first was His Honour, Justice Miles Wilson and the second was Superintendent Anne Reid.

Vulpe's lieutenant, Codrin Dalca had told him he was given a tip by a dealer that he needed to hook up with a young Chinese by the name of Andy Zhou in the CBD in relation to the fentanyl heist. Dalca had been told that Zhou would sell his own mother's soul for money and that if anyone could point Vulpe's man in the right direction it would be him. No-one had heard any rumours or stories about the fentanyl being on sold in any sort of trafficable amounts since it's disappearance from the Cleanstyle factory, so Dalca had bought some time in which to manoeuvre and keep his boss happy. Vulpe would be off his back for a couple of days.

"Through a third party, I have managed to get hold of the home address of Wilson, that self-righteous judge who sent one of my boys down for twenty years. The fact that my man is now dead is of no consequence. He was of Romanian birth so his name must be honoured. Wilson decided to ignore me and a very generous amount of money to find him innocent, so now he must pay. When I say pay, I mean pay with his life. Dinu, I want this and the next problem I am paying you handsomely for to be eliminated within a few days, do you understand? Once these are resolved I will guarantee you. safe passage back to our homeland," Vulpe said with a flat business sounding voice that didn't betray the fact that he had no way of guaranteeing his last statement.

"For the half million dollars that you are paying me, they will both be done. I do not care about both of these hits being legal people. They are the ones that put me behind bars for eight years. It will be nice to get some retribution. When do you want them done?" a stony-faced Luca said.

"I want them done within a couple of days, one after the other so the fucking police department won't know what's hit them. Wilson will be gone, and the pressure will be on Reid and her group to solve it quick. They'll be so busy with the homicide people all over them because of the supposed connection between me and Wilson that they won't have time to get organised before you hit Reid," Vulpe said as he handed Luca a small piece of paper with the home address of Wilson on it. "You can stay at Dalca's place tonight. I'll arrange for a car with false plates to be left outside his address in the morning. You can have a look at Wilson's address in Carlton and do it tomorrow night or the night afterwards." With that he called Dalca's name and waited until he came into the office after handing Luca pictures of both Wilson and Reid.

"Dinu is staying at your place tonight. Tomorrow morning he will be gone. Nothing for you to worry about. He'll be down in a minute."

"Why my place?" Dalca blurted out in a panicky voice."

"Because I fucking said so, that's why! Don't argue with me. You just get going on my fentanyl and track down who has got it. As soon as you do, and my other task is finished we will be paying whoever took it a little visit. Now fuck off Codrin and stop acting like a scared little boy," Vulpe said dismissing him with a wave of his hand.

Codrin Dalca was not about to argue with his boss, especially in front of a hit man like Luca, so he quietly walked out of the office door and went downstairs to his car to wait for the big ex-con from New South Wales.

Bogdan Vulpe went to a sliding wooden panel that was inset into the wall behind him. Once unlocked, he withdrew a chrome plated Carpati 7.65-millimetre pistol in one hand and the magazine containing eight loaded rounds in the other. He handed both to Luca with a smile on his face. The significance was not lost on his assassin-for-hire.

"A specialty of our Secret Police back home," Luca said, checking the slide mechanism before inserting the magazine into the pistol's grip with a resounding click and placing the weapon into the pocket of his jacket.

"Wilson went against me, and that bitch Reid insulted me. I think fixing them the Romanian way is just. What do you think my friend?" Vulpe said with a smile directed towards Luca.

"Very just. They will learn the hard way to disregard our heritage. When do I get paid?"

"Do you have a transfer system still available to you in the homeland?" Vulpe said.

"Yes. I still have access to an account that I haven't used in some time. You will have to wire it through," Dalcs said.

"One and a half million Romanian Leu. That's half a million Australian dollars. Give me details and it will be done as soon as I know the hits have been made.You have my word," Vulpe said, tongue in cheek. Without the money from the sale of the fentanyl which he hadn't retrieved, he knew he had no money to pay Luca. He would worry about that later.

Luca stood and headed downstairs to where Codrin Dalca was waiting nervously in his car. Luca stepped into the car and without saying a word pointed to the factory exit.

As the car turned out of the factory, a very young Constable, who had been told to pay attention to any comings or goings at the Cleanstyle factory was momentarily distracted after checking his phone for personal messages. All he saw were the tail lights of a car disappearing down the road and around the next corner. Kate McLaren had just turned around to the back seat to retrieve her lap top computer so she could continue with the day-to-day paper work of being a Senior Sergeant at the Carlton police station. Sit-off or not, the paper trail was not going away. By the time she had got back into position she looked up at the factory and saw nothing. The young Constable had quickly put his phone back in his jeans and did not want the wrath of Kate McLaren coming down on him for possibly fucking up. He said nothing.

"Anything that moves near that place, I want to know about it, understand, Constable?"

"Absolutely," the young member said thanking God the interior light was off so his Senior Sergeant couldn't see his bright red face.

Chapter 33

"It's not his fault, it's mine. I should have told him to ditch his phone as soon as he got into the car," a very sorry looking Kate McLaren said to Signorotto and the team the next morning back at the office. Nothing however was going to pacify the very angry Senior Sergeant who proceeded to rant at his fellow Senior Sergeant.

"Seriously Kate, what were you thinking? Talk about a rookie mistake. Now we don't know where Luca is. When did you realise you'd lost him," Signorotto said almost in a scream.

"Hang on Tony. Back it down a bit. What's happened has happened. There's nothing we can do about it," Vince Anderson said holding up a hand at the furious Tony Signorotto.

"It was about one AM when Vulpe drove out of the factory. All the lights were out so I guessed that if Luca was in his car he must be lying on the back seat, so I radioed for a Highway Patrol car to do a routine traffic stop while we followed. I also got a uniform car from Fitzroy to keep an eye on the factory when we took off. The Highway boys did the usual check of Vulpe's car while he gave them a mouthful. No one with him in the car and no one in the boot. They had to let him go. Went back to the Fitzroy car and on the way, the young member fessed up that he may have let a car get away while he had been checking his phone. As I said, my fault for turning away," a downcast McLaren said. "I'm not going to hang him out to dry. He should have been in uniform at the station. We are too short staffed."

"You might not hang him out to dry, but I will. He's still a copper and he should have known better to do his job, and on top of that he should have told you he'd fucked up when he knew he'd fucked up. Not fucking good enough," Signorotto said, continuing to raise his voice. Vince Anderson had heard enough.

"Enough is enough, Senior Sergeant. Go and have a coffee or something and calm down right now," he said pointing vigorously at the door of the office.

Tony Signorotto stood and stormed out of the office.

"What the hell was that about?" a stunned Anderson said looking at Tyler, McLaren and Schaeffer. "Thank Christ the Superintendent is downstairs making a phone call. You know him better than me. Is he normally like this?"

"No boss, he isn't. He's got something on his mind. He was as quiet as a mouse on the way back last night," Tyler said.

"He seems worried about every little thing at the moment. Never gone off at me or anyone before like that," Kate McLaren said quietly, still recovering from Signorotto's rant. "Even back here at the station he seems to be okay for a while but then starts double checking everything I do as though he is afraid he has missed something. If you like, I'll have a quiet word with Susie, his wife. She's a friend of mine. I'll catch her for a coffee later today if that's alright?"

"Absolutely, Kate. We need him calm and back on track. Nothing to Reid, okay everyone?" Anderson said looking around at the still quiet members. They all nodded in agreement.

"In the meantime we need to keep looking for Luca. It's no good going back to Vulpe because he's a ticking time bomb. Any stops on and we have to have some proof."

Christ, one mad cop and one pissed off crook. What next? A concerned Vince Anderson thought.

Chapter 34

Dom Santino's restaurant in Lygon Street was its usual busy place as Kate McLaren entered into the Italian style appointed establishment. She had rung ahead and made sure she could book a small table in a quiet corner. Dom had put a reserved sign on a front window table and escorted her to it.

"How is Kate today?" Dom said in his usual happy voice. He had known Kate for a few years now and Tony Signorotto and his wife Susie had been friends of the Santino family for a long time. Years ago, Signorotto had intervened in an attack on one of Dom's daughters in the restaurant kitchen. Two would-be crooks had been given a lesson in why not to return to the suburb of Carlton.

"I'm fine Dom. Susie Signorotto is joining me for a coffee." As she spoke, Susie walked through the door and beamed at her two friends. Dom held the seat out for Susie then went off quickly went off to get their coffees. There was no need for him to ask what type they wanted, because Dom never forgot his special friend's needs.

After saying hello to each other, Susie spoke. She knew that in a week or so she and Tony were catching up for dinner at Dom's with Kate and her husband Tom.

"Love having time for a coffee with you, Kate, but is there a problem? We're having dinner together next week aren't we?"

"Just wanted an off-record chat about Tony. He's just not himself the last week or so. He is so irritable and is snapping at everyone, even me. Double checking everything the sergeants do as though he's scared of losing control of the place. I'm only asking because we have so much respect for him and a few of us are concerned."

Placing her handbag on the seat next to her she looked at Kate with a sad smile.

"Tony and I have had some long chats about how much longer he's staying, not just at Carlton, but possibly in the Force. I think it's taking its toll on him. You know what it's like with him. He's full steam ahead the whole time and when he's not, it worries him. He leads from the front and reckons he's getting to the point where he has to think about life after the Force, and I have to agree with him. He's got a great superannuation scheme and I am a few years younger than him and I have no intention of quitting my job for some years yet. He and I are worried about little Grace if something happens to him. I want him in the station and he wants to be on the road as well. It's just such a dangerous job now. There is no respect for the police anymore."

Kate knew exactly what Susie was talking about. She herself had married an ex-SAS army officer whose first wife had died in a hit-run car accident. She was now stepmother to his daughter Summer.

"I thought it must be something other than the job we have on at the moment. I won't go into it and I don't know if Tony has with you, but I think it will come to a head pretty soon. I can see where you are coming from Susie. To be honest, what started out as a basic protection job for a judge who unfortunately lives in Carlton has become a bit more complex. We have a new Superintendent on board but she is from England and I don't think Tony is all that rapt with her running the show. She's certainly competent, but you know what he's like when it comes to anything to do with Carlton. It has to be his show. He has always been this big protector to everyone. We are all capable of looking after things but he just doesn't want to let go. I'll have a quiet word with Vince Anderson who is working with us and see if we can keep Tony in the background a bit and give him some time to think things through."

"That would be great, Kate. Keep it to yourself but Dom Santino has asked Tony to come into the business with him. His daughters are all going their own way now and he wants to keep the restaurant going but with some new blood. You know he thinks of Tony as the son he never had, don't you?"

"Well, that's certainly news that I won't be telling anyone," a very surprised Kate McLaren said. "Makes a change though. Most coppers retire and think only of security jobs or such. Very different indeed, but it would keep him in Carlton, that's for sure."

"Now, let's talk about something else besides the bloody Police Force," Susie Signorotto said with a laugh as Dom placed their coffees on the table.

Chapter 35

Dinu Luca was sitting behind the wheel of an old Toyota sedan outside the Carlton address of Judge Miles Wilson two mornings later. The vehicle had been supplied by Vulpe through a third party. The registration plates were false but they had been stolen off a similar year Toyota, so they didn't look out of place to even the trained eye of the Highway Patrol. The only thing a nosy cop would look twice at if he did a check would be that this Toyota was white and the stolen plates were from a yellow model.

Luca was going to do a quiet recce of Wilson's unit by checking the front entrance whilst putting pizza vouchers in the mailboxes of the five units. Most people who had "No junk mail' stickers on their boxes never objected to ads for discount foods, so even if one of the residents walked in or out while he was having a look, he didn't think he'd get an argument. People who could afford a townhouse in Carlton always appreciated a bargain.

It was just after one in the afternoon when, after having a good look at the judge's home from all sides, he was just getting back into his car when he looked up to see a late model Mercedes pull into the communal driveway and the judge himself step out of the driver's door and retrieve his mail from the box. He seemed to give the pizza offer a longer look than the Australia Post letters. As he stood there, a woman whom he presumed to be the judge's wife walk out of the front door with a surprised look on her face before speaking loudly across the driveway.

"What are you doing home so early? Haven't you got a case on today?"

The judge called back across the roof of his car that Luca

had no trouble in hearing through his open window.

"It's been adjourned. I'm just going to get changed and pop down to Brighton to see how things are going with the yacht. You want to come for the ride?"

"Where's your police sidekick? Aren't you meant to have one with you?" a concerned Helen Wilson replied.

"There's a big demonstration on in the city today. They are extremely short staffed so they asked me if I could possibly go it alone for one day. I told them I can look after myself for twenty-four hours. Fitted in well for this."

"I'll leave you to it then. I'm going up to the Nova cinema. Joan from next door got two tickets to an author's talk and we are off to listen to Anne Cleeves, the British crime writer. Love her work and we get signed copies of her latest books. You go off and annoy the yacht repairers."

"Okay. You going now?" the judge asked.

"Yes," she said closing the front door before waving to her husband and heading off.

Luca couldn't believe his luck. Wilson started his car and slowly drove down the driveway, stopping only to press the garage door opener and wait for it to go up. Luca was out of his car in a flash, pistol in pocket. As his target swung into the garage, Luca ducked under the descending roller door and walked the few steps to the now opening driver's door. Judge Wilson looked up in shock.

"Who are you?" he said angrily as he saw Luca swing the pistol towards him. Survival instinct kicked in immediately as Luca pulled the trigger a fraction of a second after Wilson struck the would-be assassin's gun hand with the opening car door.

The noise from the pistol was very loud inside the garage as the shot grazed the judge above his left eye. He grabbed Luca and struggled violently with him, tearing the side pocket from the Romanian's jacket as a second shot was fired into Wilson's chest from close range. The judge dropped immediately to the floor as blood flowed freely from his face and now his chest.

A panicking Luca reached up and grabbed the cord release for the garage door and pulled quickly on it. The door slowly began going up. He could hear voices on the other side and as his view became clearer, he could also see two pairs of legs gradually appearing. Throwing his torn jacket over his head to hide himself, he raced up the driveway past two elderly residents. The stunned men looked from Luca to the body of Judge Wilson lying in an ever-expanding pool of blood.

Luca drove off in a hurry, still shocked at the desperate fight his elderly opponent put up.

One of the residents, a retired doctor went to work on stemming the river of blood that was pouring out of Wilson, whilst the other man desperately dialled 911 for an ambulance.

Time seemed to drag, but eventually they heard multiple sirens approaching and suddenly an ambulance and several police cars all came to a screeching halt in the driveway.

After what seemed like an eternity to the judge's neighbours, he was eventually lifted onto a stretcher and placed in the rear of the MICA ambulance at the same time as one further police car arrived on the scene. Kate McLaren stepped out of this one. She saw that the judge was about to be taken away, so she climbed in to the rear of the vehicle and took hold of the judge's hands. Looking up to her with wild eyes, he grabbed her wrist and shoved a rolled-up piece of paper into her hands along with the torn pocket.

"Pocket, paper, paper," was all he could say before

lapsing into unconsciousness.

She got out of the way of the paramedics, so they could work on him, and after a couple of minutes, the vehicle disappeared with flashing lights and eerily sounding sirens. She suddenly realised she still had in her hand what Judge Wilson had shoved at her. Looking down, she saw a torn and bloodied piece of cloth and then a piece of paper which fell to the ground. Picking it up she saw a hand written note with Judge Wilson's address on it. She suddenly realised the enormity of the note.

This wasn't some random robbery gone wrong. This was a hit!

Chapter 36

Kate McLaren called Tony Signorotto on the way back to the station with the news on the attempted hit on Judge Wilson. She said nothing about the note. Prior to this she had phoned Helen Wilson and arranged to pick her up outside the Nova cinema for transport to the Alfred hospital.

An hour later she walked into the station and not only found Tony Signorotto, but also Anne Reid, Vince Anderson and Max Tyler. She approached Tony but could see he was on his phone but held up her hand with the note hoping that he would discontinue his call, however, she was answered with Tony holding his phone to his chest and speaking to her.

"Be with you in a sec, Kate. I'm on the phone to Chi Quang at the Asian Squad."

Kate quickly realised that although she had become so used to the idea that Tony was her direct boss, being the Senior of the two of them, in actual fact he was third in line in the Task Force. Above him were Reid and Anderson. As she turned, Reid called her across.

"What's happening with Wilson?", Reid said impatiently knowing that McLaren had ignored her in the first instance. "The Senior Sergeant has been on the phone ever since we got here. I want answers so I might as well start with you."

Kate McLaren then gave Reid and Anderson a complete briefing of the attempted hit and made sure she included the fact that she had arranged for a member from Prahran to stand guard at the hospital.

"What makes you think it's a direct hit on Wilson? It

could have just been an armed robbery gone wrong," Reid said with a clipped tone.

Kate was about to tell them about the note but was cut short. As she began to speak, Tony finished his call and joined the group. Reid held up her hand for Kate to stop.

"You are first Senior Sergeant. Let's get a bit of order back here, What do you have to say?"

Tony himself was on edge from the phone call and could see that Kate was not happy about having Reid's hand held up in her face. He wasn't about to let his fellow Senior Sergeant down.

"Kate looks as though she has more important info for us. Tell us about Wilson?"

Reid exploded. "Senior Sergeant, I think we had better go into your office before we continue," she said pointing across the room. Tony raised his eyes to McLaren and followed Reid into his own office.

"Listen to me, Senior Sergeant. You call me in here and for the last twenty minutes, not only do I have to wait for you to get off the phone, but then when McLaren comes in she goes straight to you even though she can see you are busy. Both Inspector Anderson and I are totally ignored. Then when I ask you to speak you ignore me and ask her to start talking. I am the Superintendent here and I run the show."

Tony Signorotto had come to the end of his patience. His mind was trying to concentrate on the job at hand but was crowded with thoughts of possible retirement and other things, mainly the future of his family. He stepped past Reid and slammed the office door then stood between it and Reid.

"Look here, Superintendent. Kate and I have had each other's backs for a long time now and to be honest I want to hear what comes out of her mouth before what comes out of yours. You might not have thought much about tipping Vulpe over the edge by wiping your shoes on him, but that act is partially why we are here now. You might be an expert in terrorism back home, but it means shit here when we are dealing with home grown inner Melbourne mafioso. You need to shove your rank crap too and let us help you fix this situation. Like it or not, you know nothing about Melbourne and even less about Carlton. Stop pulling rank and get your act together by listening to what's important and not to who's the higher rank for Christ's sake. I'm sure Vince Anderson knows that Kate and I know more about the local crooks than he does and he's not trying to outdo anyone. If you want this solved let me run it. You can have all the kudos at the end and look brilliant in front of the Chief if you like. Then you can piss off back to England and get another promotion. Don't get me wrong, Superintendent. I just want Vulpe. You can have the limelight. Now how about we go back outside with smiles on our faces and listen to Kate and then I'll tell you what the Asian Squad has to say. I am running on fumes at the moment. My tank is about dry, so if you are thinking about putting me on paper for what I have said then go for it, otherwise let's go and get Vulpe and sit down and have a drink when it's finished." With that, he quietly opened the door and returned to the group who were standing together looking anywhere but at him. It was about sixty seconds before a shell-shocked Anne Reid walked out of the office and spoke quietly.

"Senior Sergeant McLaren, what information have you got for me. Sorry, for us I meant," she said looking at Tony Signorotto.

Kate proceeded to tell the others about the shooting of

Judge Whelan and the fact that she believed it was a hit on him directly. Tony let that fact hang in the air waiting for Anne Reid to say something.

"Kate, what makes you say it was a direct hit?" Reid said eventually.

Kate McLaren then produced the note from her pocket. "This is what the judge handed to me in the back of the ambulance. It has his address on it. It was together with this," she said producing the torn jacket pocket. "It doesn't take much to come up with the fact that the judge tore the jacket pocket from his assailant and with it his own addressed piece of paper. Whoever shot him had been given the address. I know I've jumped the gun a bit here, but I've already rung the Homicide Squad and they are getting over to the hospital."

The Task Force members looked at the note without speaking as the reality of what it meant sunk in.

"Excellent work, Kate. Initiative, that's what I like," Reid said giving a half smile towards Tony Signorotto. "Tony, I want you and Vince to lead from the front on this."

"First things first. We need to know if that handwriting on the note is Vulpes' or not," Vince Anderson said.

Max Tyler spoke straight up. "Easily done. Give it to me and I'll have it checked next to his writing on his bail forms."

"Right, Max, you get onto that right away," Anderson said to the young detective who took the note from Kate and started to head out the door before being suddenly called back by Signorotto.

"That phone call I got was from the Asian Squad. Apparently a wannabee Triad boy has crossed the line and given us a big tip on the fentanyl heist. He has it that Yang Chen and a couple of his heavies grabbed the shipment and killed Anton Funan in the process. Story goes that Chen is on his own now because of the killing and also the huge unknown factor around the fentanyl. This guy found out through a Triad senior who he is related to. Apparently Chen has tried to do a deal now with the Triad because even he has found the shipment to be too hot, but the old Triads won't touch it. Looks like the Triad have backed Chen into a corner and now no-one will touch him, which probably suits the older ones down to the ground. Some senior ones agreed to inspect the shipment but only to find out where it is. They want him gone along with the fentanyl, thus the leak down to the junior mouth. The phone call gave me the address."

"So basically, the Triad want us to go and clean it all up. They get us out of their faces and get rid of Chen. A real win-win situation I suppose," Max Tyler said.

"Tony, your thoughts?", a now contrite Anne Reid said.

"They won't be leading us up the garden path, ma'am. Solves all problems except our mad friend Vulpe, but if we get a search and seize warrant for tomorrow morning and clean up the fentanyl side then we can just concentrate on him."

"Correct. Leave the warrant with me. Vince, get things organised with the SOG for an early morning raid. Kate, you get some sort of Operation Order together. Max, I want that writing checked and Tony to sign off on the Op Order along with his Asian Squad contact. I also want a twenty-four seven guard on Wilson and the same for his wife until Vulpe is nabbed. What time in the morning shall we hit Chen?" Reid said turning to Tony.

"Four AM sounds like a plan. What do you say, Vince?"

"Good to go, crew," Anderson said as McLaren, Tyler and Anderson moved away, which left Tony Signorotto and

Anne Reid looking at each other. Tony went to speak.

"This is so different from leading a team back home Tony. I suppose I need to learn the differences. Let's hope this all goes to plan." Tony looked at her before speaking quietly.

"The plan is only as good as the team ma'am and you have a good team here. Trust me, but there is also something else we have to consider. If Vulpe was mad enough to try and get a hit done on Wilson, it stands to reason that he might come after you. He will be like a cornered dog when he finds out, and he will find out, about his fentanyl shipment being taken. I want you covered wherever you go. Apparently Wilson didn't have any police guard with him and that's not happening again. I want Chloe Schaeffer with you everywhere and I don't care what upstairs says, you are also having a Force Response Crew tagging you everywhere and baby-sitting your house," he said quietly.

"One thing with this raid, Tony. What does this Chinese informant have to gain from telling us about the fentanyl location. You'd think he would want some sort of return favour from the Asian Squad wouldn't you?"

"Good point ma'am, but I suppose he is just an underling doing what he is told by the Triad."

"Maybe, but it sounds like we may be doing their dirty work for them. We'll concentrate on the fentanyl first. A good bust like that will go down well with the top floor. That's a headline act, Vulpe is just another crook," Reid said walking away with a devious look on her face.

Tony Signorotto couldn't believe what he had just heard.

Just more braid looking for promotion, he thought.

Chapter 37

Andy Zhou wasn't a person to let an opportunity of this size pass him by. He had already passed on his Triad uncle's information about Yang Chen and the fentanyl to the Asian Squad member, Chi Quang via a contact. Little did anyone know that his next step was to let Chen know that the information had been passed onto the police. The perfect double cross which would hopefully end up in a firefight with Chen losing. That would leave a big drug vacancy to be filled. Andy Zhou knew how he could fill that hole: with himself!

Zhou was a small player who ran around the extremities of the Melbourne Triad, being at their beck and call both day and night. He was sick and tired of being given 'scraps from the table'. He had established quite a flourishing drug trade away from the prying eyes and ears of his family. His one fear was coming face to face with Yang Chen. He had already had one run in with him over a client that both he and Chen were supplying, unknown to each other. When Chen found out that Zhou was supplying to the same person, it ended up with Zhou spending the next week recovering from a severe beating at the hands of Chen's associates. Since the fentanyl theft though, combined with the murder at the factory, Chen's men were starting to jump ship. They were getting more scared every day with the fentanyl unable to be sold on, along with Chen's fanatical ways. They all knew the local Triad had put out the word about Chen and the shipment. They knew what was good for them and had been quietly advised to walk away from the madman. Zhou just wanted Chen gone either way. Arrested or killed was fine by him. He could then start to build his own empire.

Zhou had informed the Asian Squad and didn't care if Chen found out. He wasn't worried about retaliation because he didn't care about his family at all. His uncle had been holding him back for years, treating him like a servant. He knew one Chinese runner who had managed to get away from Chen after the murder at the factory and now wanted to work for him. The request had been met with approval, but only if Zhou's new employee could get the word back through Chen's remaining loyal workers that the Melbourne Triad had let the Asian Squad know where the fentanyl was and that a raid was imminent. He knew from experience that Chen would never give up the fentanyl without a fight and would now be paranoid about the fact the police were onto him. Exactly what Zhou wanted — a fight to the death.

Zhou had his newest member text Chen on a burner phone with the information that the Triad had 'foreclosed' on Chen. Now it was just a matter of sitting back and watching the fireworks. He didn't know when the police would raid but he knew it would be soon.

The fact that Zhou knew that the Police would be going in cold, not knowing that Chen had already been told about their raid did not worry him in the slightest. All Zhou wanted out of this was Chen permanently out of the way. He had no interest in the fentanyl or the lives that would be lost. He was building up a thriving industry with the younger generations of Chinese who were after designer drugs.

Unlike his peers who loved the fireworks spectaculars that took place over Chinatown on a regular basis, Zhou just wanted one big explosion — Chen's factory! Hopefully the surprised look on the faces of members of the Asian Squad at the raid would lead to a few of them being eliminated also. The more the merrier.

Chapter 38

While the members of the Task Force concentrated on their various jobs that day, there was one thing that Anne Reid could not get out of doing. She was locked in to proceeding with an interview for the drive time slot on radio station Double R that evening. It had been advertised heavily by the station and there had been a lot of feedback about the upcoming interview. Radio station Double R was located in the Docklands with its frontage on a very wide footpath.

She had promised the radio station owners, one of whom was a close ally of the Chief Commissioner that she would allow herself to be interviewed about the new world-wide trend of cross-country policing, especially in relation to international crime gangs and the importing and exporting of drug shipments.

Reid couldn't deny that in the short time she had been with Vic Pol that this topic had become extremely relevant to the Task Force she was heading. After all, she was from the United Kingdom and was up to her English eyebrows in trying to stop a large-scale drug shipment hitting the streets. Although there was no way she could talk specifics, she could go a long way to warning off listeners that were in the drug trade or those who thought about it that if you wanted to import into Victoria then you would suffer the consequences. She would have given anything to be able to talk about her current situation but for the sake of future court cases she had to keep quiet. She had briefed the Crime Department and the investigating Homicide members about who she and her team now believed was responsible for the shooting of Judge Miles Wilson.

Max Tyler had checked Vulpe's bail forms along with a member of the Forensic laboratory from Macleod. There was no doubt that the handwriting was the same on both the bail forms and the note that Kate McLaren had returned with.

The day was buzzing by with preparations for the dawn raid on Chen and Reid was confident that she had left the preparation work in the correct hands. She now had to finalise the search warrant at the court and then get down to the radio station for the five o'clock interview.

Stepping out of her office at Police headquarters, she rounded a corner and ran up against a fully armed Senior Constable Chloe Schaeffer together with another even more fully armed member of the Force Response Unit. Reid knew it was useless to argue with them about her safety and underneath it she was rather pleased that Tony Signorotto, along with all he had to do today, still managed to organise the two members for her. It would make her look very important when she stepped out of her car at the radio station. In fact she was going to have the Force Response Unit member stand inside the foyer while she spoke.

"Okay, people. First job is to get me to the Melbourne Magistrates Court to finalise the warrant we need. Turning to the FRU member she continued.

"Senior, have you been briefed as to why you are with me?"

"Yes, ma'am. I have had a quick look at your itinerary for the two places today. The first is a bit of a maze inside the Magistrates Court building but I have already briefed the Senior Sergeant in charge of the Protective Service Officers there and we will be amongst friends.

The second one is a bit dodgy but once you are inside it

should work out. We will park directly outside the front door and I will take you in while Senior Constable Schaeffer here minds the car. Same coming out."

"I think it will look good if I enter the building with you all dressed up in your camo gear and assault rifle."

"Ma'am, you're the boss. I've been told to give you close personal protection. I don't care what I look like."

"No offence, Senior but perception is everything."

Chapter 39

Bogdan Vulpe's world was starting to change very quickly. He knew once he had let Dinu Luca loose to seek out Judge Wilson, there could be no turning back.

Vulpe wanted to let people know that he was not some small fry to be wiped off their shoes, or more importantly not some person to have their shoes wiped on! He was after all, to his way of thinking, the most important Romanian in Melbourne. What he didn't realise was that the Italians, Greeks and even Chinese that were in the same drug dealing business as himself couldn't have cared less about who some of them referred to as the Cleaning Man, a reference to his cleaning business.

The fact that the Cleanstyle Industrial Cleaning Company was a successful legitimate business never made Vulpe realize he didn't need to deal in drugs at all. The trouble was, he came from a background of crime in Romania. He had been brought up in a family of criminals and he was actually proud of it. He truly believed that to be a Romanian crime figure was something to aspire to.

Unbeknown to Codrin Dalca and his other employees, he had successfully sold Cleanstyle to a well-known Melbourne based industrial cleaning company for over five million dollars in the past week. Along with that sale he had also negotiated very good sales for his other legitimate businesses along with his house for a lot more. Vulpe was hell bent on revenge, but he wasn't stupid. He had to pay Dinu Luca with small change and also pay his suppliers for the stolen shipment of fentanyl. He realised that he could take a hit with these two debts from the sales, but he had made up his mind that he wanted to return to his roots back overseas.

Now that the hit had been done on Wilson, he had no intention of returning either to his house or to his old factory. He had flown his wife back home and was himself booked on an overseas flight in two days' time. He just had one more thing to do and that was to seek revenge on that bitch of a female police officer.

He had arranged for Dinu Luca to meet him in a suburb that he had only driven through. Toorak. While he sat in The Husk café in Malvern Road and thought about his exit from the country and setting himself up back in Romania, his mobile rang. Looking at the screen he saw that it was Codrin Dalca. Vulpe had it planned in his mind what he was going to say to his now ex-employee.

"Dalca. What do you want?"

"What's going on? Where are you? The factory is locked and I have the staff waiting outside," a panicking Dalca said.

"Well, Codrin, I have sold the business. You can tell the ones waiting there that unfortunately there is no guarantee the new owners will continue their contracts of employment. I have decided to return to where I can conduct business with my countrymen. I have made arrangement for everyone to be paid up until the end of the week, but that's it."

"That's it! What do you meant that's it? There are people here depending on the cleaning contracts," Dalca said before lowering his voice and continuing. "You know I have other types of deals happening with shipments that have nothing to do with cleaning products. On top of those I am trying to track down that certain 'package' that went from the factory a while ago. What am I going to do now? Or are you just going to play the hitman with your new boy Luca?" he screamed down the phone.

Vulpe spoke with a reasonably controlled voice. "Listen to me Dalca. Just forget about Luca because he hasn't finished his work for me yet. Forget about any shipments from now on. I will be re-routing those myself once I am set up back home. I will deposit a bonus into your account but I dare say you will have to look for another job because after all, I asked you to track down that fentanyl and you have come up with a big fat zero. Luckily with the money from the businesses and my house I can cover what I owe and still be comfortable. That's all that matters to me. I don't give a stuff about people who can't help me, Dalca!"

"You seem to forget that I know all about your fucking mad revenge plots. Word is out that there has been a hit on a certain judge we both know. Thing is though, my spies tell me that there is a police guard on a high-profile member of the legal fraternity at the Alfred hospital. Looks like you didn't finish the job, Bogdan. You want to play with people's lives then look out you prick," a livid Codrin Dalca said before turning off his phone without waiting for a reply.

Vulpe's train of thought was fast becoming a train wreck. In any other moment in time, he would have had Dalca kneecapped for speaking to him like that, but he wasn't even thinking about him. His mind was reeling with something that he hadn't considered and that was that Judge Wilson was still alive. While he was contemplating this scenario, Dinu Luca walked into The Husk and sat down opposite him. Speaking very quietly, he smiled at Vulpe as he spoke.

"I need payment for that hit," he said with a straight face.

Vulpe leant forward on one elbow. "What went wrong?"

"Nothing. It was a clean hit. It's fixed. No problems with that old man."

"Well then, how is it that he is still alive in hospital?"

"Impossible. He went down like a bag of shit. Who said he was still alive?" a white faced Dinu Luca replied quickly.

Vulpe knew that Codrin Dalca had a lot of people 'on the ground' that he listened to and dealt with because of all the dealing in the day-to-day world of drug dealing. If he was going to believe him or his new associate Dinu Luca, then it would be Codrin Dalca every time.

"The person's name is of no concern to you but I take it to be true. You have one last chance to make things right. You have to go to work tonight and finish that female cop. Then you will be paid for that. You can forget about being paid for the first one. I pay for jobs completed, not fucked up, understand?"

Luca was desperate for a big pay day, because he also wanted to get back to his homeland but at the moment had no money. He couldn't argue with Vulpe so he swallowed his pride.

"Why does it have to be tonight?"

"Because she is giving an interview at a radio station tonight about international crime and what this state can do to prevent big time drug dealing. Well, as far as I'm concerned she is going to be treated like some big-mouthed cop in Mexico. Over there they kill them as soon as they open their mouths about drug enforcement. I will let her give a talk about how good she is in her job and then I will show this fucking state how good I am at mine. You are going to blow her away as soon as she steps back outside the radio station," Vulpe said as though he was talking about stepping on an insect.

Dinu Luca didn't care if it was a cop or a judge, but he knew he had to get this one right otherwise he would never get home. There was no international extradition treaty between Romania and Australia, so he just had to make sure she was dead before she hit the footpath and that he could get to the airport as quick as possible.

"You know I want to get back home so can I use some of the money to buy a ticket to fly out of here tonight? You can transfer the rest of it electronically to my account back home," Luca said with a pleading look in his eye.

Vulpe thought for a moment and realised it was probably the best way to do it.

"Where do you want to fly to tonight?"

"Anywhere in Europe. I have my passport and I can get back home from anywhere over there quickly."

Vulpe reached into his briefcase beside him and pulled out his laptop. Minutes passed before he found a coach class ticket that would take Luca from Melbourne to Frankfurt with one stopover in Doha with Qatar airways. It was scheduled to fly at nine o'clock that night. He spun his laptop around and showed Luca the details.

"Best I can do," Vulpe said.

"Do it. Take the money out of my payment and wire me the rest when the job is done. We have a deal?" a desperate sounding Luca said.

Vulpe had no intention of crossing Luca because unbeknown to the hit man, they were both headed back home and he didn't want to be walking through the beautiful streets of Bucharest and be gunned down by Luca because he hadn't paid up.

"We are both Romanian. A deal is a deal," Vulpe said as he bought the ticket through a shell company attached to one of his fake on-line businesses he had set up for just such a purchase. If there was a paper trail, he would be back home in a day or two so he didn't worry about it. It would take the police a lot longer than that to figure out that the trail went around in a circle and back to his old cleaning business. Minutes later the deal had been done.

"Now let's get down to business," Vulpe said, handing Luca a set of keys to a Ford Mondeo that he had paid a snitch to steal that morning and park in an alley nearby. "I will tell you exactly what will happen later on today. I have already done a recce of the outside of the radio station and I suggest you get down there with plenty of time to spare to do your own. This bitch will be arriving by four thirty because she is on the drive time slot. She will probably come out about six. Sit in your car and listen to her give her views on crime. She should appear back out five or ten minutes after she has finished. Keep an eye on who is with her so you can plan her exit. She will most likely have some office bound lackey driving her. It shouldn't be a problem. Hit and run," a smirking Vulpe said, not knowing that Vince Anderson and Tony Signorotto had also done their homework.

Chapter 40

The momentum with which the bullet struck Anne Reid in the chest as she left the radio station after her interview threw her backwards across the footpath away from the car door which had just been opened by Chloe Schaefer. The Superintendent struck the concrete light pole and slumped to the ground, blood pouring from her.

Schaeffer dived across Reid's body in an automatic reaction to protect her boss at the same time as she heard the second shot. The pain that tore through her skull was indescribable. Suddenly on top of the shot she heard, there was the cacophony of a burst of automatic gunfire. Schaefer's ears were ringing, but at least the gunfire had stopped suddenly but the noise of a screaming man continued the confusion along with the unmissable smell of gunpowder.

Rolling off Reid's prone body, her eyesight disappeared as blood flowed freely down her face from what she vaguely thought was a severe head wound. Trying to get to one knee, vertigo hit her quickly and she toppled to the ground next to the person she had tried to protect. Not only had a red mist descended over her but suddenly a veil of blackness overtook her as well. All went quiet.

***

It was hours later when Chloe Schaeffer opened her eyes and suddenly wished she hadn't. Lightly touching at her head, all she could feel was a cloth bandage that seemed to cover the entirety of her skull. Her head pounded and she knew she was about to be sick. Without knowing where it came from, a bucket appeared in front of her blurry eyes and she proceeded to vomit for what felt like an eternity. Upon finishing she collapsed back onto the pillow of her hospital bed. The sight of Max Tyler's face at first confused her but then after a short time comforted her. This was a totally different scenario to the last one she could remember. Putting her hand back to her head, she winced in pain.

"Hey, take it easy. That bandage is there for a reason. The same reason you have had all your hair shaved off. Count yourself lucky that you are alive and that you still have the opportunity of marrying me at some stage, lovely lady," Max said quietly as he reached across the bed to hold her hand.

Chloe replied with a raspy sounding voice.

"All I remember is diving across in front of Reid. She was thrown across the footpath and hit a light pole after being shot. I'm so sorry I couldn't save her. The shooter aimed for a head shot and got it," the still shocked police officer said as she began to sob.

Max Tyler leant down, gently holding her head with both hands just as Tony Signorotto came into the room with Vince Anderson and Kate McLaren.

"A Valour Award coming up for another female at Carlton by the looks of it," a smiling Signorotto said to Chloe's tear-stained face.

"Don't talk to me about medals, boss. I just wished I could have saved her, but there was blood everywhere by the time I got to her. She didn't move."

A bemused look crossed over the faces of the members who had just arrived.

"Haven't had the chance to talk about the shooting yet. She doesn't know," Max Tyler said, holding up his hand before any of them said something.

"Don't know what?" came the immediate question from Schaeffer.

"Superintendent Reid is alive, Chloe," Signorotto said. "That blood you saw on her face was from where she hit the light pole. Just very bruised."

"But she was shot. I heard a shot and then she just went backwards," the stunned police officer said.

"Yes, she was, but she had the good sense to take notice of what your Senior Sergeant here said to her before she went to the radio station and that was to wear body armour under her dress tunic. She had on a ballistic vest, Chloe. She must have just forgotten to tell you about it," Vince Anderson said.

"She's actually down the corridor now getting checked over for the bruising that the round caused when it hit the vest. Beside that she'll be okay. I've just been with her and she wants to come and see you as soon as she gets the all clear. You're the one who has come off second best," Kate McLaren said with a smile.

Chloe Schaeffer slumped back on her pillow and looked at the ceiling before sitting up again to speak.

"What happened after I passed out? The last thing I remember is hearing automatic fire, probably from the Force Response member."

"He got him as he jumped into a car on the other side of the road. He shot the front tyres out and called for the shooter driver to get out. He gave him plenty of yells and warnings to raise his hands and get out, which he eventually did, but it ended up being suicide-by-cop," Anderson said.

"How?" Chloe said.

"He got out after about sixty seconds of banging his head on the steering wheel and shouting something about getting back home to Romania. When he stepped out he raised his weapon and took aim at the Force Response member. He might as well have brought a knife to a gunfight as they say. The member dropped him with two shots to the chest before he could fire his pistol. He was dead before he hit the ground. There were a few civilians who saw the confrontation and have backed our guy to the hilt. They all say he gave the crook heaps of chances to surrender but it looked as though he wanted to go out in a blaze of glory. Ended up being gory but not glory. "

"Do we know who he is?" Chloe said as she put one hand to her head and winced.

"Yeah. The same guy who we photographed at Vulpe's factory. Hit man by the name of Dinu Luca. Not long out of Supermax in New South Wales," Anderson said.

"Pretty obvious that Vulpe had put him up to hit the judge and the superintendent, but now that he's dead we can't interview him," Signorotto said. "Would have been good to dump Vulpe straight into it."

Chapter 41

With Chloe Schaeffer in hospital and Anne Reid confined to bed with what turned out to be a broken nose, the remaining members of the Task Force were now flat out preparing for the raid on Yang Chen's mini fortress in Barkley Street, Brunswick East very early the next morning. They were working in conjunction with their fellow members from the Asian Squad, led by Chi Quang.

As the Operation Order was being put together by Kate McLaren using the Special Operations Group together with the Dog Squad, Tony Signorotto, Vince Anderson and Max Tyler were in deep discussion with Quang in an upstairs office at the Carlton Police station over details of the raid when a Senior Constable knocked on the door.

"There is a person downstairs who wants to speak to you Senior Sergeant," he said looking directly at Tony Signorotto.

"Pretty busy up here at the moment, Senior. Can you just take a message and I'll ring him back," Signorotto said, half turning to the member before looking back to Anderson.

"Sorry boss, but he reckons you'll want to speak to him right away. His name is Codrin Doolca, Dilca or something."

"Was it Dalca?" Signorotto said spinning around in his chair.

"Yep, that's it. Dalca, Codrin Dalca," the Senior Constable said.

The Task Force members looked quickly from one to another before Max Tyler jumped up.

"Get downstairs mate and don't let him go. I'll be right down," he said as the member turned to leave before Tyler spoke to the others.

"I think we may have a bit of evidence that ties Vulpe to Luca. I got a phone call from the people at forensics and they confirmed that the writing on Vulpe's bail form was the same writing that was on the note Judge Wilson grabbed off his attacker whom we now believe to be Dinu Luca. Vulpe's our man, I'd say."

"Let's see what Dalca has to say about his employer. Bring him up Max," Anderson said.

Minutes later, Codrin Dalca was sitting with a resigned look in front of the members of the Task Force.

"What is it you want, Dalca? To be honest, now that we know that the Black Knights are no longer in the picture with the fentanyl, I don't think you can be of much use to us," Anderson said.

"Word travels fast when a cop is shot. I can tell you all about the shooter," a desperate sounding Dalca said.

"We know all about him, Dalca. His name is, or was, Dinu Luca. Apparently hired by your boss Bogdan Vulpe to get rid of a couple of top law people in this State. We just have to get a bit more evidence other than what we've got and then you and he will be arrested. We know where you live and you're not the most important thing going on around here today so you might as well go on back to your work and start sweating. Seeing that he has escalated the stakes to shooting judges and police, what we had with you is now meaningless. Cop killers, or should I say attempted cop killers come first. We'll get to you, don't worry," Signorotto said before Dalca spoke again, stunning the whole room with what he said.

"I will give him to you on a plate, Mr. Signorotto. I was in the office with him and Dinu Luca when Vulpe told him he wanted *one bitch copper and one fucking judge knocked.*' He made me arrange the firearm for Luca also. I told him he was mad and that he should just think about the fentanyl and forget any revenge shit on those two. He was obsessed with it. Now he's sold the legit cleaning business and left everyone out of work. What do you want from me, because I'll give you everything you need on that bastard."

Silence engulfed the room before Tony Signorotto finally spoke.

"You give evidence against Vulpe in court and we will look at putting you and your family into witness protection to keep the Romanian mafia from you."

"They won't do anything to me, Mr. Signorotto. Vulpe has no friends in the mafioso and now that he's tried to kill the cop and the judge they will abandon him and any of his ideas completely. I just want my family protected."

"Max. Get his statement down in writing right now and arrange for his family to be picked up and housed somewhere until we get Vulpe. Unfortunately, we have to get this fentanyl raid out of the way first," a worried sounding Anderson said.

Dalca suddenly spoke. "Even with my contacts I couldn't find the location of that fucking fentanyl shipment. Can I ask how you did?"

Chin Quang took over when he heard what Dalca said. "I got a tip off through a Chinese fizz. Why?"

"Why would a Chinese fizz tip you off so you could arrest another Chinese? No matter who you are raiding, the Chinese Triad will not put up with a rat in the ranks. You should know that. Doesn't matter at the end of the day if the Triad like or dislike him, an arrest is losing face. Any Chinese will want to go down fighting. I have dealt with them over a long time now and they hold honour above everything. I would say your so-called fizz will be having a bet each way."

"I was thinking this morning that the information was given a bit freely," A red-faced Quang said to everyone.

"Your fizz will be someone outside the Melbourne Triad and wants to climb the ladder. Be very careful. Odds on, whoever it is your raiding will know you are coming. He won't give information for no gain," Dalca said looking from person to person as suddenly a light bulb moment appeared in his desperate mind.

"You can kill two birds with one stone here if you're smart," a stony-faced Dalca said to the room in a loud voice, but not to anyone in particular.

Tony Signorotto had met plenty of players like Codrin Dalca before in his police life and as far as he was concerned they were only ever after two things. The first was making money and the second was saving their own skin. He was guessing Dalca was chasing after the second but Tony was not going to give him something for nothing.

"I know what your game is here, Dalca. You just want to feed Vulpe to us to save yourself. The best you are going to get is a stint in the can while your wife and kids hit the witness security merry go round."

"I know I'm going to do time. All I want is my family safe and to do my stretch anywhere but where Vulpe ends up. Give me that and I'll give you Vulpe," Dalca said.

"How are you going to do that?" Max Tyler asked.

"Do we have a deal first?" a now nervous Dalca replied.

Tony Signorotto looked from Tyler to Quang and saw Tyler look at the man who would have to authorise the deal, Vince Anderson.

"Up to you, Detective Inspector, but you are basically setting up an illegal sting. Think about it."

"If we take Vulpe, then he will end up in Supermax inside Barwon State. You will go down for a few years on low level drug dealing because you will plead guilty, that's a given, okay? Sale prison is more likely your home for a few years. Your family will be re-located, that I can guarantee. Tell us now and take the deal or shut up and you just might share a cell with your Romanian mate."

Dalca remained silent for only a few seconds.

"Vulpe hasn't paid his distributors back home for the fentanyl shipment as far as I know. That's big money. Selling his business and whatever here will get him cash to help fix that but it won't leave him anything else. What he needs is that fentanyl shipment money real quick. All I need to do is let him know where it is and he'll drag in a few favours with some low-level scum to get it back by surprise and force. You could sit back and watch the fireworks between him and whoever has it. Rather than going in and risking a shootout, I could get him to go in first and you could pick up the pieces."

"That shipment is worth millions. If you've fallen out with him why would he deal with you again?" Anderson said.

"Simple greed. He was pissed off with it being taken but he'll want it back if he can get it and sell it. It will set him up. I'll do a cash for location deal. I'll hit him up for say, two hundred and fifty thousand in advance and then give him the address. That amount won't mean anything to him with his ego running wild thinking about getting it back. What do you say?"

"Could give us both Vulpe for the attempted hits and the fentanyl and get us Chen into the bargain," Chi Quang said quickly as he and Anderson nodded to each other.

Tony Signorotto was not going along with it. "Dangerous and wrong, Inspector. You are setting Vulpe up in a possible crossfire." Anderson was not listening to him.

"You make the phone call and tell him that tomorrow

night is the night to hit. We'll be listening. That'll give him a chance to get his shit together and find some dudes to help him. Thing is though Dalca, you're not leaving our sight till after this is over and you are in remand. Okay?"

"I'll ring him now on my mobile. He'll wonder what the fuck I'm doing after he dropped the business sale on me."

"This is way out of whack, Vince," Signorotto said. "It's one thing us going in after the fentanyl but putting Vulpe in it too is madness. If he gets killed or even wounded or hurt while the raid goes on around him and it comes out that he was there because we let Dalca do a deal with him we all end up in the shit. Don't do it."

"Make the call, Dalca," Vince Anderson said with a gleam in his eye.

Chapter 42

Bogdan Vulpe realised suddenly that his chances of flying out of Melbourne back to his homeland had taken a big hit. Dinu Luca had made sure of that. He was now in a fight for time.

The Police might have been able to hide the fact that a judge had been shot at his home because after all, the average punter wasn't interested in the legal system when it came to who was who in the court system. The shooting of a cop in front of passers-by on a footpath in the busy city was a whole new ball game. It was all over the news as Vulpe sat in the back of a little coffee shop in Moonee Ponds about to sip on a macchiato when his phone vibrated on the table in front of him.

He paused the cup before he drank as his brow creased, seeing Codrin Dalca's name appear on the phone. He let it ring out. Ten seconds later it vibrated with an SMS message. *Fentanyl found. Answer your phone if you want to get it back.* Thirty seconds later the phone vibrated with Codrin's name flashing again. This time Vulpe answered it before it rang three times. Dalca got in first.

"Don't ask me how I found it. Just be aware that if you want it the cost is two fifty, and I'm talking two fifty with four zeros in my account in one hour. Got that?" Dalca said in the room full of police.

Bogdan Vulpe thought quickly and realised the outlay versus the income. It would be a plus on his side of the ledger.

"This is the only deal we do Dalca. We are finished. Who has it?" he said angrily.

"Let's say the Chinese, but not Triad. Put the money in

and ring me back. I won't fuck you around. It will give you enough time to get some of your scummy mates together and pay a visit. It isn't far away." Dalca said.

"How do I know I can trust you, Dalca?"

"Trust. Trust! You should talk. I have thirty of your now redundant workers who need money to live. They trust me so you fucking can as well," an even angrier Dalca replied.

"Alright, alright," Vulpe said. I'll do it, but you'd better not be fucking me around, Dalca because I'll get you knocked," an angry Vulpe replied.

Codrin Dalca couldn't help himself with his reply.

"You'd never do it yourself you prick and you don't have any friends left here in Melbourne after you dumped your fellow Romanians, so just do it. Get back to me inside the hour." Dalca then hung up.

Vulpe pulled out his laptop and put it on the Formica table then scrolled through to his various banking sites before deciding to raid his least profitable. He would have another coffee before he transferred the money. He didn't want to look as eager as he felt.

Twenty minutes later and after he had completed the transfer, his phone lit up with an SMS message giving the supposed address of the fentanyl. He had to take the message as the real deal because even Dalca knew that somehow he would end up a dead man if he had given him a false address. Now it was time to take back what was his.

Working the phone furiously, Vulpe managed to come up with a sure-fire plan. He quietly laughed to himself after he arranged to meet his new helpers outside the Pullman Hotel in East Melbourne the following night. Back to the Black Knights!

***

The Task Force members had been hanging off every word that Codrin Dalca had said to Bogdan Vulpe in the phone call. Signorotto, Tyler and McLaren had all voiced their disapproval of it. Vince Anderson knew he was treading on dangerous ground by allowing Dalca to make the call because he was letting a person who was about to be charged face serious injury or even death. There had been earnest discussion amongst the members before he authorised it on behalf of Superintendent Reid after a phone call had been made to her by Anderson. When Codrin Dalca had been taken downstairs awaiting the charge sheet, Vince Anderson got the group together.

"We will have to get Vulpe as soon as he gets to the fentanyl location. The last thing we want or need is a confrontation which we can't shut down quickly because it could end up a three-way fight between the haves and the have nots regards the fentanyl and us in the middle. Tony, I want you and Max concentrating on the streets around the premises and I will head up the raid along with the Special Operations Group. Superintendent Reid and I have talked long and hard about it, now let's get to work. First things first though, Tony and I will do a drive by of the premises and get back here as quickly as possible. Max, I want you downstairs getting Dalca settled into his cell. A couple of charges before a Justice of the Peace will do for now. Once we have all this other stuff under wraps we will tie up the whole package."

Anderson and Signorotto headed off to do the recce of the premises.

Wonder what that long and hard talk was about, Signorotto thought.

Chapter 43

"Did you hear me?" Vince Anderson said this time with a slightly louder voice as he drove the unmarked police car towards the address where the fentanyl shipment was located. There was no recognition from his passenger Tony Signorotto. Anderson dabbed the foot brake a couple of times causing both of them to be jerked back and forth in their seats.

"Are you with me on this Senior Sergeant?" a now annoyed Anderson said loudly as he looked at Signorroto.

His passenger shook his head and looked at Anderson.

"Sorry Vince. Things just seem to be happening so fast what with one thing being the fentanyl and the other being Vulpe. Just trying to think, that's all. By the way, why did you bring this car. It just stands out like dog's balls being a Toyota with an obvious police aerial on the front. My little daughter would pick out this car. Hope there's no one looking when we cruise by, that's all. I still say its madness involving Vulpe in this. We can get him another way."

"Nothing else bothering you mate?" Anderson said with concern, thinking back to Signorotto's recent mood swings but totally ignoring his comment about his choice of vehicles.

"Juist thinking back on times in Carlton, Vince. We've always had a drugs problem around the place but we could more than not handle it quickly amongst ourselves. No offence to Anne Reid but I just don't like the idea of anyone just sliding in sideways and running the show. It's not her, it's just the way things seem to be going now. New ideas are okay but what happens overseas should be policed by that particular country. They don't know the crooks here no matter how much they say one drug dealer is the same as the next. It was a bad move by her wiping her shoe on him. He's one bloody mad Romanian who now has a grudge to bear. Now we are in the situation where we have her off because she was shot and we have one of my people in hospital. I would have handled things differently, Vince."

Vince Anderson thought long and hard before he replied. At the end of the day, no matter what he thought about the business of cross-country policing, he was stuck with it and he not only wanted to support his Superintendent, but underneath it, he also wanted some kudos if they got the fentanyl. It would be a major points score for promotion later on.

"Tony, you come from a different era of policing. Not that you don't fit into this era, but in times gone by, people used different methods. New ways aren't necessarily wrong."

"Yeah, I don't disagree with you on that but these cross-border policing situations tend to ignore what is a lot of times, some very good local knowledge. That's why I always not only have weekly sergeant's meetings at Carlton, but I also have a lot of one on ones with the guys and girls that hit the streets every day. The hardest worker in this job isn't some flash harry detective, it's the uniforms on the front line every day. Local policing should be kept local, not be given to a person who just wants ideas that they can take back to their own country and leave us with their ways of doing it. I just wonder where we are going with it all. I'm telling you, this raid needs a lot more planning and the involvement of the people upstairs."

"You sound a bit disillusioned, mate?" Anderson replied.

"Not disillusioned, Vince, I'm just starting to query where I fit into it all. There are somethings that never change with the people like the Vulpes of this world. They know only the old school type of policing. Call me a dinosaur if you like but there's an old saying about policing and it's stood a lot of the old guard in good stead."

"Okay, play your card. What's the saying?" Anderson said shaking his head slightly.

"People sleep peacefully in their beds only because rough men stand ready to do violence on their behalf."

"Did you photograph that on some cave wall somewhere, Senior Sergeant? It's all about community policing these days. Keeping people informed and happy about their surrounds and their community."

"If you believe that, then you are sillier than the rest of them in town. Try telling some member at your local community gathering that the reason we couldn't stop their nice Volvo being stolen from outside their equally nice home because we were too busy turning on our body cams and waiting for some dickhead Police Communications civilian to run and get permission from some equally dickhead manager to make a couple of these shitheads *do the chicken* instead of getting away with the car while we stand around looking like a bunch of boy scouts."

"Boy, have you got your angry pants on today, or what, Tony?" Anderson replied as he slowed to peer at the premises they were after.

"I just hope this operation to get two birds with one stone as you say, doesn't turn pear shaped. Thinking on it seriously Vince, I reckon we should just send the SOG in to this place and get whoever is in there together with the fentanyl and concentrate on Vulpe another day. In hindsight, I don't like splitting the Task Force with one half going after it and the other half going after Vulpe. Might look good on paper and I know you decided how it should be run, but did you really or was there some influence from Reid because she reckons it would be more efficient use of troops and this is the way it would be done back in the UK?"

"This is the way she wants it. End of argument."

"Just doesn't sit well with me. I hope the right hand that's looking after the raid part knows what the left hand Vulpe part is doing if they both collide together."

"Worry about that if it happens, Tony," Anderson said in a dismissive tone as his head turned from side to side as he looked the building from inside the car.

"Too much influence from a third party who isn't going to be there on the night," a concerned Signorotto said. "Mark my concerns down please Vince."

"Duly noted, Senior Sergeant," Anderson said without telling him about Reid's intentions.

Tell it to the Coroner when it all goes wrong. I'm getting too old for this shit! Signorotto thought as a shudder ran down his spine.

Chapter 44

Tony Signorotto arrived at the Carlton Police station early on the morning of the planned raid. Vince Anderson and he had done a recce of the small factory premises on Amess Street in North Carlton the day before, only to discover that the target was surrounded by residential houses either side and across the street, which made for a far from ideal situation. There was a small roller door entrance and a front door which was steel framed and very strong. Signorotto did not like it at all and was concerned that Anderson was possibly thinking of this raid as a 'feather in his cap' moment regarding his career.

This thought was running through his head as he entered the Task Force room to be confronted by two people in deep conversation as they stood over a council set of street plans. One of these two was Vince Anderson and the other was a seemingly recovered Anne Reid. Signorotto was momentarily taken aback by the sight of the Superintendent. Before he could speak, Vince Anderson beckoned him over as other members of the Task Force started entering the room.

"I think we have this pretty well down pat here, Tony," Anderson said looking up.

"Who is 'we?' Vince," Tony said lowering his bag to the floor and looking directly at Reid.

"All of us of course. The Task Force," Reid replied tersely.

"When did you come back on board, ma'am? Thought you'd be off on the injured list for a while like Chloe Schaeffer," Signorotto said with a touch of sarcasm in his voice.

"Probably the old British stiff upper lip. Inspector

Anderson has been keeping me up to speed. I'll be overseeing this little soiree tonight, broken nose and all."

Signorotto could feel the tension rising in himself. "Yes, I suppose an actual bullet wound like Chloe's would keep you down for a bit longer unlike your bruising and nose. Bravery medal coming up for that girl don't you think?"

Anne Reid stood up and looked directly at Signorotto. Vince Anderson stood with an ever-increasing red face.

"There's an old saying in the Met, Senior Sergeant when it comes to bravery awards. *Always follow the Officer's advice. No points or medals for stupidity.* Girl should have had her vest on. I don't want to embarrass her by putting her up for a medal when she could have got herself shot."

Tony Signorotto's next words would go down in folklore at the Carlton Police station.

"She did get fucking shot, Superintendent. She got fucking shot protecting you and now you won't even put her up for an award. That the way it's done back in England, eh? All for one and one for one?"

Vince Anderson stepped between Signorotto and Reid.

"You'll apologise right now, Senior Sergeant for that comment."

Kate McLaren and Max Tyler were listening to every word being said.

"There will be no apology from me, Inspector. It is obvious that with your plans here, you have made your minds up without me or other members of the Task Force. I expressed my concerns to you yesterday about this raid. There has been no input this morning from me, who is the best expert on premises and their surrounds in Carlton and it looks like you are going to go ahead and expect the SOG to fall into line with everything. Do I not get a say in things on my own patch?" a now furious Tony Signorotto exploded with.

As Vince Anderson went to reply, Anne Reid intervened.

"You will be on the exterior perimeter watching for Bogdan Vulpe, Senior Sergeant and that is all. Inspector Anderson has already expressed his concerns about your suitability regarding your position here at Carlton. I think as the only officers here, we know best. I will not worry about your comments regarding some stupid bravery award till after this is all over. Then and only then will we talk disciplinary action. Tonight, Inspector Anderson and I will lead the raid and you can take care of the perimeter along with Sergeant McLaren and Detective Sergeant Tyler. Hopefully between the three of you, Vulpe will be apprehended."

Tony Signorotto smiled to himself before speaking. "To start with, are you going to give any of the surrounding residences a forewarning of tonight's show? Have you arranged any next door or backyard surveillance before it kicks off? How do you know this Chinese guy is in there and even more importantly, have you been in contact today with the Asian Squad about who may be in this place. More importantly, what is the rush? Get the plain clothes boys to sit off it for a day or two and watch the comings and goings. You could end up shooting some Asian food delivery guy or a bloody Uber driver. This has not been planned properly I'm telling you. Or is it a case of both of you backing each other up in some 'bound for glory' scenario. A climb up the ladder for you, Inspector and a big pat on the back for you when you get back home, Superintendent and tell everyone how you re modelled the policing landscape here in Melbourne?"

Max Tyler quickly pushed Signorotto away from the two officers before he could say more. Kate McLaren, however, was not to be outdone as she turned towards the two stunned officers with palms outstretched.

"With all due respect, Tony has exploded because you haven't really consulted him in regard to this raid. You only had a quick look at the outside of this place and you haven't even got the Divisional Response Unit to monitor it. Who knows what's going on inside or even who's inside. If that shipment of fentanyl is worth so much it could have an army looking after it for God's sake. This factory could have an upstairs hook and pulley set up, the old type for hoisting up goods at the rear. You are only looking at street plans. Carlton is a very old suburb with heaps of architectural oddities. This place needs more time to be reconnoitred. Seriously, you need to listen to Tony."

Anne Reid stepped into Kate's space and looked at her directly. Kate returned the stare.

"I cannot believe the disrespect shown to myself and Inspector Anderson here today." This will be taken further. Go and do your job Senior Sergeant or I will replace you."

You're so right, Tony. Bound for Glory these two. God help us! Kate McLaren thought.

Chapter 45

"Pull out of it, Tony. Don't go on the raid tonight," a worried Susie Signorotto said to her husband as they sat in Dom's restaurant in Lygon Street drinking coffee.

Tony had told Max Tyler and Kate McLaren where he was going after the blow up with Reid and Anderson. He hadn't even had time to change into his uniform before his day had come crashing down. He wasn't about to continue the argument so he headed for the watering hole that was the second home for all the troops at Carlton. On the way, he had rung Susie to meet him. Talking was the only way he was going to calm down.

"Phil Stone wouldn't have gone along with this the way it is. Reid and Anderson are going in half-cocked even though they have the SOG. The boys from the DRU should have been sitting off this place all day today to see who comes and goes. They would have crawled all over the joint and given us the feedback we need," he said to Susie who had been his sounding board for years. The fact that this job was going down the same night really worried her.

"Is it just the fact that you don't have enough details about the building?" she replied, hoping that what she was saying was helping her clearly worried partner.

"It's more than that. Reid has had Kate write up an Operation order for basically a frontal assault on the place and I know from an inquiry that I made, the SOG are only going to be given their job at the briefing tonight at seven o'clock. They aren't happy that they've been kept out of the loop. Brett Clark, the Inspector who is leading the SOG tonight has told Reid in no uncertain terms that the whole plan has huge holes through it. He was told to toe the line.

This overseas policing method where everything is just decided by the Superintendent on the night, who by the way will be safe inside her car is crap. She has me and Brett and won't take advice from either."

Before Susie could reply, both Kate McLaren and Max Tyler walked in the front door. Kate had put an old denim jacket over her uniform shirt. Both walked up and sat at the table. Dom Santino, the long-time owner and friend to all in the navy blue approached.

"Coffee and biscotti coming up. I know you have important things going on here because it is a long while since any of you have come here without smiles on your faces. I have a feeling that something that is not good is in the wind, as you say. Whatever it is just stay safe my friends. You are my family too, remember."

"Thanks Dom. You know what we think about you and your family and this place. Lygon Street would never be the same without you," Tony said.

Turning towards the kitchen, Dom suddenly swung back and pointed a finger at the table.

"Never be the same without you, Tony. You remember that also," he said seriously.

Tony turned back to the others who had just walked in.

"What are you two doing here? Kate, you should be getting that Operation Order up to the Commander's office in town to be signed off on. Max, you should be liaising with Chi Quang and the Asian boys about their role tonight," a slightly bemused Signorotto said.

"We told Anderson that we were going for a break seeing that we are going right through till after the raid and that as soon as I got back I'd get the Op Order uptown. Bloody Reid cut him off and grabbed it, signed it and said that her signature would be enough. She added that's the way it's done back in London. No need to take it up the tree apparently," Kate said in a low voice.

As Signorotto opened his mouth in disbelief, Max Tyler chipped in.

"She doesn't want Chi or his group doing anything. You wouldn't believe what she said," Tyler said.

"What? What did she say?" Signorotto said.

"That she didn't trust Chi or his squad and that they were probably in cahoots with the triad and any other Asian dealer."

"What the fuck? Did she say that in front of Anderson?" a disbelieving Signorotto said.

"No, she was talking out loud to herself and didn't realise that I was close by. She's nuts this woman. Won't go along with any known methods we use here. She's a one-man band.

Unbelievable. She's just after a big drug raid result which will put her name in lights and probably get her a promotion when she pisses off back to England. She hasn't even talked about our part trying to get Vulpe. Anderson is just riding her coat tails hoping for a big pat on the back. Our bit is a sideshow. If Vulpe turns up, which I think he will and he gets a sniff of her being there, he'll go off like a bomb," Tyler said.

"The fact that she hasn't even put the Vulpe situation into the Op Order is totally irresponsible. Susie, you might want to get going because Kate, Max and I are going to have to get our heads together now and basically do some brainstorming for our part," Tony said.

"Tony, can I see you by the door for a minute please?" Susie said with a degree of concern in her voice. Tony got up and walked with his wife to the door.

"I'm no expert on police matters, Tony, but even I can see

that this is fraught with danger. Can you get out of it at all?"

Tony took his wife by both arms before he spoke.

"I would if I could but Reid knows I won't leave Max and Kate do this alone. She has sidelined us completely. I think Anderson is like a deer in the headlights and Reid is driving the car with the headlights on full beam. I have to look after my own here, Susie. It'll be okay, I promise," Tony said before giving her a hug and seeing her out the door. He walked back to the table where Dom had placed a tray of coffees and biscotti.

"Time to get our own plan up and running guys. Got any ideas?"

"Vulpe doesn't know the raid is going on so he'll be wanting to do his own one to get the stuff back," Max Tyler said. "He knows how big the shipment is so he'll have to have help and he'll have to have a van of sorts and wait for dark. What about we tie up both ends of the street and divide and conquer?"

"What's the plan if we split up?" Kate said.

"Boss, how about you and the DRU at Amess and Mary Streets and myself, Kate and some uniforms at Amess and Park Street? If we can get hold of two Traffic cars from Dawson Street, one at each end then we should be able to contain him from either end. I don't think even Vulpe would take on that many members," Max said.

"I can arrange the DRU and the Traffic boys but we'd better not forget that this guy is trying to get back a million dollars' worth of gear that he had taken off him. He is an angry guy at the best of times and if he thinks he can get past us he will try to. Just keep him away from that other shit show that Reid will be running. I think it's probably the best we can come up with," Tony said.

"Yes, let's just have each other's backs and keep out of their way," Kate said.

"Okay, we'd better get back to the station in an hour or so. Let's just talk this through and I'll make some calls for assistance from here," Signorotto said picking up his mobile while the other two reached for their coffees.

Chapter 46

Yang Chen was starting to worry about the fentanyl shipment he had stolen from Bogdan Vulpe on the night he killed Anton Funan. He thought there would be a quick reprisal from the Romanian when he found out that it was Chen who took it, but he had no idea that Vulpe was as much concerned about revenge on the judicial system as he was on retrieval of the fentanyl.

Chen had been sourcing possible buyers for the shipment but he was having trouble dealing solo. When any potential clients started negotiations, they believed he was acting on behalf of the Melbourne Triad. The fact that he wasn't caused several buyers to try to gain points with the Triad by telling them what Chen was up to. The older members of the Triad sat back and smiled. The simple fact of life in Melbourne was that you dealt through the Chinese Triad and not some Chinese try hard. They were quite willing to let Chen slowly hang himself with no sales whilst waiting for Vulpe to reclaim his shipment. If truth be known, the Melbourne Triad was not interested in an untried drug which would bring both state and federal police forces stampeding to their door.

Whilst holed up in his North Carlton factory with his wannabee apprentice drug mules who saw Chen as the new wave of Chinese dealers, Chen was becoming paranoid about any vehicles or people that stopped within the vicinity of his bolt hole. He had some serious CCTV cameras covering not only the entire premises but also a long distance one that could pick up registration numbers up and down Amess Street for some distance and would immediately notify him of any vehicle that stayed too long outside. He knew all the local cars and was only interested in anything that looked like vans or unmarked police cars. One that morning had made his radar ping. He took a photo of it and immediately reached for his phone and rang a well-paid contact at Vic Roads to get the details of it. Within minutes he knew it was an unmarked police car. His radar was now beeping on high alert.

Chen had received a text stating he had been sold out by the Triad. He didn't know that the real culprit was Andy Zhou, a nephew of a senior Triad member. The Triad itself wasn't in the business of texting people. All Chen knew was that the police were onto him and now he had a fight on his hands. The other unknown part of the puzzle was that Chen didn't know that Bogdan Vulpe had also been given his location and a time to hit.

Chen had the firepower to defend the factory and a handful of zealots to go along with him.

A calmness overtook his thinking. *In the midst of chaos there is also opportunity.*

He had previously cut the shipment into ten packages that could be easily transported on motor bikes. He was quite willing to do deals for any amount of the fentanyl and deliver it to wherever in or around the city for an additional fee. The next move was to load four of the bikes with half of the shipment and get them out of the factory before the inevitable raid. He had placed trackers on each bike so he could tell if they had reached their four destinations, which were various free parking bays at suburban railway stations. They would be parked amongst many other vehicles for twenty-hours maximum before they raised any suspicion from nosey Protective Service Officers. The remainder of the shipment he would pack onto another motor bike. If he worked quickly he would get them all away immediately and if there was a raid late in the night then he would be saved. He quickly grabbed his cohorts and set them to work presuming that if there was a raid it would be during darkness. It was time.

Chapter 47

Johnny Petran and Mick York from the Divisional Response Unit made a habit of never letting Tony Signorotto down if they could help it. When they got the urgent call from him to be in position early at Amess and Mary Streets in North Carlton there were no questions asked. They knew they would be given all the information they needed before they got to the location.

It was about five o'clock in the afternoon when they got to the intersection and parked where they could see the front of the suspect premises and in particular the small roller door that led onto the street. Johnny Petran had been taking notes over the phone from Max Tyler while Mick York had been driving. Tyler had told him who they had to keep an eye out for, but Petran told him not to bother with a description of Bogdan Vulpe as there had been many a run in between the DRU and Vulpe and his associates over the years. Johnny and Mick were more than keen to sit and watch anyone or any car that approached the factory. They parked their unmarked Ford SUV, complete with a serious bull bar attached, in a position where they could stop any suspect vehicle very quickly.

About twenty minutes later, Tony Signorotto jumped out of another unmarked Police car as it pulled up next to the DRU vehicle. He was in full uniform and carrying not only his issue Smith and Wesson Police and Military Special nine-millimetre pistol but also a twelve shot Mossberg 590 pump action shotgun. His ride continued on to the next intersection of Amess and Park Street with its two occupants, Max Tyler and Kate McLaren. Signorotto jumped into the back of the DRU vehicle. Johnny Petran smiled as he turned to his long-time friend.

"You loaded for bear, mate? That's a serious looking shotty you've got there."

"I've got a bad feeling about this gig, boys. As I told you on the phone, this bloody English Superintendent and her side-kick Inspector are going for glory here. This Operation has been basically cut in two now and I want to get Vulpe way before her and the poor bloody SOG ended up in some sort of fire fight over the fentanyl shipment. They don't know who or how many are inside or what firepower they are coming up against. Reid has basically cut me adrift to look after the Vulpe part. I even made a phone call to the Deputy Commissioner for Operations about stopping this but he's tied up all day in meetings," Signorotto said, exasperated and angry.

"Hear around the traps that she likes to do everything like she did back home. People in her own office have tried to tell her it's like comparing soccer to Aussie Rules. Two totally different types of football. She's pretty gung-ho from what I've heard," Mick York said turning to Tony.

"Absolutely, but let's all just get our part done. I'll stay with you and the others can cover the end., Don't know if the traffic boys can make it yet. Aren't any rostered-on till six o'clock," Tony said.

"What time are the Superintendent and the others going to raid this place?" Johnny Petran said, pointing towards the factory.

"Seven o'clock is what the Op Order said. Be dark then. I just want my end all tucked away beforehand. Vulpe is a madman and it wouldn't surprise me if he turned up anytime, even in daylight."

Petran, York and Signorotto set themselves on alert mode, not knowing when Vulpe would show or if he had backup with him. Kate McLaren and Max Tyler did the same at the next intersection.

It was now a waiting game.

"If Vulpe wants that shipment back he will have to come in something bigger than a car or SUV. I'd be backing some sort of small van, that is if it hasn't been cut into smaller packs," Petran said quietly as his eyes continually looked up and down the street.

Tony Signorotto was re-checking his weaponry when he looked up in surprise, seeing the roller door of the factory go up and four large motor bikes being ridden out onto the footpath before two of them suddenly turned towards his car and the other two went off in the other direction before the door came down suddenly. They were past the police cars at Mary Street and Park Street before the members could do anything.

Mick York fired up the unmarked car and was about to head after their two bikes when Signorotto put his hand on his shoulder and spoke.

"No Mick, no. Waste of time chasing them and we leave this end of the street open. Get on to Kate and Max and tell them to stay where they are."

Johnny Petran relayed Signorotto's instructions then turned around after receiving a reply through his ear piece.

"They've got one uniform car with them but no one had a chance to go after them either. They're staying where they are."

"Don't know what all that was about but we have to concentrate on getting Vulpe. Someone might want us going off on a tangent but we only have one target at the moment, and he has yet to show up," Signorotto said whilst thinking to himself.

"That was too planned to be a random thing," the

experienced Johnny Petran said slowly.

"Exactly what I was thinking, mate," Signorotto said slowly putting the shotgun back on the floor of the car as his mobile rang shrilly. All the screen displayed were the letters UC. Signorotto answered it immediately. "What's going on?" Signoroto said, never asking who he was talking to. He knew it was the Sergeant-at-Arms of the Black Knights, Pete English.

"I'll be quick. Your man Vulpe has picked up two extras for tonight when he tries to get back his fentanyl. He's selling straight to us for a discount on the proviso that we give him a hand getting it back. I hear from a source that a few of you and the boys are in place and are going to stop him?"

"Thank Christ you told me, mate. Any idea of time or type?"

"About to get into the transport. White Hi Lux van. Him and two of us. This is obviously going to be my last gig with you know who. This load has to be stopped. I'll take care of my offsider and you lot can take Vulpe. I'll do a runner then."

"Any idea of which way you're coming in?" Signorotto said quickly.

The line went dead.

Chapter 48

The Sergeant-at-Arms of the Black Knights was more than happy to sit in the back of the van with the other bikie driving and Vulpe in the front. He hadn't even bothered to ask the Romanian if he was armed because he wasn't going to give him a chance to use whatever type of gun he had.

Once they pulled up at or near the factory he would be pulling out his own weapon of choice which was a Reuger 57 low recoil semi-automatic pistol. He was running through a plan of attack in his mind when Vulpe spoke.

"We're about to turn into the street where the factory is. We just go in and take what's ours, understood?" he said very quickly.

Rick Waters knew a cokehead when he spotted one and this was what worried him right now.

"How many lines have you done today, Vulpe?"

"None of your fucking business, bikie man. Just follow me," Vulpe replied as he pulled out a semi-automatic pistol from the back of his waist band. The driver started to slow the vehicle as he turned into Amess Street, one block up from Amess and Mary Street, at the same time looking Vulpe up and down.

"Hey, I didn't sign up for a shootout man. Put that pistol away. If this guy we're hitting can't be convinced by bikies and threats then I'm out of here," the driver said as he slowly drove towards the factory.

Vulpes' eyesight was good. He spotted the unmarked police car immediately, but before he could tell the driver to stop or back up, the big Ford had driven out onto the roadway behind them.

"Keep going and quick, the fucking cops are here," a

panicked Vulpe shouted at the driver who put the pedal to the metal, but to no real advantage. The Ford followed immediately but one look through the windscreen saw another unmarked police car leap out at the next intersection cutting them off and leaving them trapped in the middle.

"Now you earn your cut. Get out and start shooting. We can still do this," the delusional coked up Romanian said as pushed the driver out of the door and scrambled out the other side completely forgetting Waters who was ducking down in the back seat.

Signorotto jumped out of the unmarked police car after it had come to a stop about twenty metres behind Vulpe's white van. He was about to speak when Vulpe raised his weapon and let off two shots which only narrowly missed Signorotto.

Vulpe wondered why the driver wasn't shooting at the police, so after letting off the first volley he turned to look at the bikie who stood there with his hands in the air.

Vulpe lost all focus and any sense of reason. Again, he was being let down by people and he was going to do something about it. Without any hesitation he turned his pistol on the surrendering unarmed bikie and shot him through the head.

Signorotto raised his shotgun but Johnny Petran let go with two rounds as he stepped from the unmarked Ford. The first missed but the second caught Vulpe across the shoulder, swinging him around and out of sight behind his van. Petran, York and Signorotto couldn't believe what had just gone down. They stared from one to another but kept their firearms focussed on where they thought Vulpe to be. All three slowly surrounded the van.

"He's gone. He's fucking gone," York said as he looked

under the van at the same time Rick Waters called out.

"Don't shoot. It's me, Tony, Rick Waters," the undercover cop yelled from inside the white van.

"Come out, Rick. Come out slowly though. We don't want any more surprises," Signorotto yelled back as Waters slowly opened the sliding door and put his feet on the roadway next to the body of his former bikie mate.

"Christ, what happened?" he said looking down at the bikie with part of his skull missing and blood pooling slowly around the remainder of his head.

"Vulpe turned his gun on him when he saw your offsider put his hands up to surrender. Instead of going after some Romanian madman drug dealer, we now have a murderer on the loose. I've got to get onto Reid and stop this drug raid so we can concentrate on finding Vulpe," Signorotto said looking up and down the street in a fruitless attempt at locating the now on-the-run killer.

"We'll get the scene cordoned off and get onto D24 to get more units around here. Have to call in the Homicide boys also," Petran said as he threw a roll of blue and white police crime scene tape to York that he had got from the back of their car.

"You do that and I'll ring Reid," Signorotto said walking away and putting his shotgun back into the police car after unloading it. He grabbed his mobile phone and pressed Reid's number as the DRU boys began working on the scene.

As Signorotto went to ring Reid, Kate McLaren and Max Tyler pulled to a halt in their car after coming down from the next intersection.

"We heard three shots from here. What's happened?" Tyler said urgently.

"One from Vulpe into that guy's head, indicating the dead

male lying in his own blood on the roadway, and two return shots from Johnny. One missed but the second one winged Vulpe. He's taken off on foot," Signorotto said quickly as he put his hand up to stop any more conversation because Reid had picked up the call. He walked away from the scene to speak to her privately while the rest of his team covered the body with a tarpaulin and moved the second police car into a position to block off the intersection.

Within what seemed like minutes, two solos arrived and took charge of the traffic side of things.

As Kate McLaren and Max Tyler briefed another traffic car to proceed with caution and patrol the area, Tyler turned suddenly to look at Tony Signorotto who was yelling into his phone and waving his left hand around in the air.

"I don't think things are going too well with Reid on the phone, Kate," he said pointing towards the yelling Signorotto.

As they stared, Signorotto put his phone back in his pocket and literally stomped towards them. Before either of them could speak, he put up his hand to stop them and spoke.

"That stupid bitch has already come in the other end with her storm troopers and is about to hit the factory. I told her to stop and get the SOG into the search for Vulpe but she won't. She's determined to go ahead. She's got a fucking homicide scene here and that takes precedent. She has totally lost the plot and I'm going up there to see her. You lot stay here and take care of this mess," he said angrily as he walked off towards the factory site.

"Take your shotgun with you, boss," Kate yelled to him.

"I'd be tempted to use it on her if I did," he said raising his hand in the air in a sign of futility as he kept walking.

"She's out of control," Kate said. This is turning into a real shit show. We have a killer on the loose and she won't let the SOG look for him. He's around here on foot somewhere, for Christ's sake."

Please be careful, Tony. You're so angry it means you're not thinking about your own safety, Kate thought to herself as she stared at the disappearing figure walking towards the drug raid scene.

Chapter 49

Bogdan Vulpe was crouching behind a brick front fence in Amess Street trying to stem the flow of blood from his left arm with an abandoned T shirt he had found on the road after he ran from the scene of the shooting.

The cocaine he had snorted prior to getting into the van with the bikies was starting to wear off and he shook his head trying to figure out if he had actually shot one of them or not. He carefully held the pistol he was carrying in his right hand and ejected the magazine from the butt. It should have had fifteen shots in it but as he counted holes in the side of the magazine, he could only see thirteen rounds filling the spaces. Two were missing. Quickly pulling the slide back, one round fell to the ground. That made fourteen. Looking around, he realised the fifteenth was missing. Suddenly his memory hit back with vengeance. He clearly saw in his mind the bikie holding two arms in the air then suddenly falling to the ground with blood and grey matter bursting from his skull. He knew then that his life was either going to end with surrender or in gaol. One would lead to the next anyhow.

Hiding behind the fence, he looked up when he heard and saw police vehicles pulling up. As he picked up his weapon in preparation to throwing it onto the footpath in what would be his inevitable surrender he couldn't understand why the black clad police officers were all headed to the other side of the road and not towards him. He didn't know for sure if he had killed the man but he knew he had used a head shot from close range so the possibility of the bikie surviving was negligible. Suddenly his eyes widened when he saw who was stepping out of one of the cars. It was that bitch policewoman who had wiped her shoe on him. The same fucking bitch that had, according to his delusional mind, started all his problems. If she thought that she would get her hands on his fentanyl without a fight she would be sadly disappointed. He would die before she could do that.

After tying the old T shirt around the flesh wound, Vulpe settled down to take in the scene before him. The SOG Lenco Bearcat armoured rescue vehicle rumbled into position between his hiding place and the front of the factory across the road and Reid and her offsider stepped to the corner of the monster, both with their backs to him.

Fate had placed two things before him,.The first being his fentanyl shipment and the second being Reid. In reality though, Vulpe knew he couldn't have both. The fentanyl was basically now out of his reach, so it came down to the other gift from above and his mind was now made up. This bitch was going to die where she stood.

***

Inside the building, Yang Chen was being just as delusional there as Vulpe was being on the other side of the road. He had expected to be raided by the police, but he hadn't given any thought to the fact that this shipment of drugs was not an ordinary one. He wanted to sell it, but he knew in his mind that somehow, the Melbourne Triad had spread the word that there would be no buyers. This load was too new and too hot to handle. It would bring too much attention to everyone and that was exactly what was happening. Chen wanted to be on the top of the crime world but he had wanted it immediately. The Triad was never going to let that happen. Chen had anticipated a raid by the Major Crime Squad, but not the SOG and he realised that he had to make a quick exit via the back door so he could live to fight another day. He had firepower but the sight of the armoured police vehicle made him realise he would be fighting a losing battle. The loss of his other henchmen would be of no consequence to him. As he ran to the last motor bike that carried the biggest part of the drug shipment, he heard the police bullhorn shout out a warning from in front of the premises.

All inside are to put down their weapons and come out with their hands out to their sides.

Chen heard the sound glass shattering from upstairs and realised that his offsiders were now about to enter a gun fight with no possible hope of winning it. As he opened the rear door and saw he had a clear exit to a back alley, he didn't realise as he bumped the motor bike over the concrete door pad that his phone had dropped from his pocket and bounced onto the path. He jumped on the bike and started to accelerate when he turned around to see what sort of lead he had on the police he could hear thumping their way to the rear of the factory and saw his phone lying behind him. The phone had the tracking app on it for finding the other four motor bikes that had half the fentanyl shipment on them.

Chen spun the bike around and accelerated back to the phone. Time was now his enemy.

***

Tony Signorotto raced up to Superintendent Reid, grabbed her by the shoulder and spun her around just as the sound of shattering glass came from the factory.

"Stop the raid now. Vulpe has just killed someone up the road and is here somewhere. Get these SOG members back here and start looking for him. He is armed and dangerous," he yelled at Reid and Anderson who was standing beside her.

"I told you to take care of that part of the operation, Senior Sergeant and you obviously haven't. Well that will be the subject of a meeting later. I have already told the SOG to commence this raid. Vulpe is your problem, not mine," a furious Anne Reid said.

"You started the problem with him and now look at the situation. Stop the raid now. Get your fucking priorities right and stop thinking about how good you are going to look when this shit show is over. You two are just out for glory," he said looking between Reid and Anderson.

Before Reid could answer, the sound of automatic gunfire came from the broken upstairs windows of the building. The SOG returned fire immediately. Reid, Anderson and Signorotto stood behind the Bearcat as the shots began to ricochet off the beast.

Nothing was going to stop what was about to happen.

Chapter 50

The moment Yang Chen decided to retrieve his phone from the pathway he was in a race with the devil. The devil being the black clad SOG member that came around the corner of the building brandishing a Remington pump action shotgun.

Chen balanced on the motor bike and reached down with his left hand to retrieve the phone. Whilst trying to keep his balance, he made the fatal mistake of letting his right hand reach out in the opposite direction. In that hand he was pointing a semi-automatic pistol in the direction of the police member. It might not have been pointed exactly at him but it was waved in his direction.

A fraction of a second after the member called for Chen to drop his weapon and the same member not hearing any reply, he pulled the trigger on his shotgun, discharging the military grade buckshot from the barrel. Yang Chen was sent to Tian, or Chinese heaven, in an instant. His body was lifted off the motor bike and thrown backwards onto the concrete pathway with a bubbling red mass erupting like the lava from a volcano from where his chest had been seconds before. He was dead before he hit the ground and even before the motor bike front wheel stopped spinning like a roulette wheel as it lay between Chen and the phone he never got the chance to pick up. The SOG member pulled the slide on his shotgun, ejecting the spent shell and then immediately pulled the slide forward again to insert the next round. The shotgun never moved off the now inert form of Chen. When the smoke had cleared, only one voice was heard and that was after the member had done a thorough visual sweep of the area. On his radio, the calm and clear voice said.

"Armed suspect down and permanently out of the game. Situation under control."

The SOG member waited for his comrade to appear behind him and then removed the firearm from next to Chen's hand. He circled the area on the ground with chalk in relation to the location of the weapon and then he stepped backwards and repeated the procedure with the phone. Both items were tagged and bagged as evidence. Chen's body lay on its back gurgling noisily as body fluids kept slowly rising from his chest, nose and mouth.

***

At the front of the building, the firefight was only coming from one side. Chen's followers were still letting rounds fly towards the SOG members on the ground while Reid, Anderson Signorotto and the SOG Senior Sergeant sheltered behind the Bearcat.

"Just keep firing up at them. Get your men out there and do your job, Senior Sergeant," Reid said with a panicking and scared voice.

"This plan was never going to work. This is stopping now. I am calling all the boys away. I am only going to use the vehicle for entry and I am taking over the scene," the furious SOG leader said.

"I will tell you what to do, Senior Sergeant. You will not tell me, do you understand?" Reid replied loudly.

"I'm not telling you anything. I'm stating what is going to be done. They are my troops and you can stand there and listen to the radio call. Now get out of my way, lady," he said as he stepped around her and spoke into his radio.

"SOG 210 to all units. Retreat to a safe location and wait for instructions from me and only me. I want no more shots fired at this stage. Do you receive?"

Six separate team members replied in the affirmative.

The odd angry shot was still coming from the upstairs windows but even Chen's rear guard seemed to have lost most of their appetite for a gun fight. The SOG leader indicated for the Bearcat to retreat out of sight as all the senior members walked behind it.

"You will be charged with disobedience, Senior Sergeant. We could have all this finished now," a furious Reid said. "You have not heard the end of this."

Vince Anderson stepped up to Reid and spoke.

"The SOG is correct in this ma'am. There was no end in sight with bullets flying everywhere. This factory is too close to residences for my liking also."

"So I now have the situation where my Inspector and one of my Senior Sergeants are disobeying me and another one here, namely you Senior Sergeant Signorotto has failed in his mission completely. This will all go down on paper and as far as I am concerned you will all end up in front of a discipline board."

"This isn't the High Seas, Superintendent and you aren't some bloody admiral snapping orders from the bridge of a fucking warship. You have lost the plot completely," Signorotto said, looking at Reid in amazement. "Anderson, take over for God's sake!"

Vince Anderson knew in his mind that the situation need to be brought under the control of the SOG immediately. He stepped up to the SOG commander.

"What do you want to do?" he said.

"First off, get that Superintendent out of the way. Secondly I want everyone back to the other side of the street. I am sending the Bearcat in. It can take out that roller door and then my boys can go straight in and up. We are not going to stand here being fired upon indiscriminately."

Anderson nodded to the SOG commander and then turned to Reid.

"I am taking over the perimeter command here now, ma'am. Step back to the other side of the road now," he said indicating to the red-faced Superintendent who turned on her heel and walked away muttering threats. Signorotto walked to the far footpath as the Bearcat moved slowly moved forward to the roller door.

Let's get this done quickly, Signorotto thought.

There was someone else who was thinking that also, but he wasn't in a blue uniform!

Chapter 51

The Bearcat armoured rescue vehicle went through the roller door like a knife through butter. By the time the door was demolished, the SOG members had stormed through into the ground floor of the factory and within one minute, they had done a sweep of the entire area. The word *clear* resonated throughout the floor six times, which accounted for all the office space and the common area. The only space that was to be cleared now was the upstairs where the members knew there were at least two shooters. The SOG commander grabbed a bullhorn and surrounded by his team, stood at the base of the stairs and called through the speaker.

"This is the Police Commander. You will all put down your weapons and come down the stairs with your hands in the air. Your boss, Yang Chen is dead. If you look out the rear window up there you will see his body on the pathway. If you decide to keep fighting, you too may end up dead. Come down now."

All members had their weapons trained on the stairwell. The sound of footsteps going over to the back of the upstairs floor could be heard. The shooters upstairs were obviously checking on the whereabouts of Chen. Screams from one person to another could be heard. The voices then seemed to become loud argumentative before silence overtook the top of the stairwell.

The highly trained SOG troops never lowered their weapons or took their sight from the floor above. Minutes passed before a broken English voice sounded from above.

"We no fight. We stop."

The SOG Commander called back.

"How many of you are there?

"Two. Only two."

"Throw all your weapons down the stairs and come down with your hands above your heads."

Within seconds, two AK 47 assault rifles came clattering down the steel staircase followed closely by two semi-automatic pistols. These were followed by two young Asian men with their hands raised. Two members removed the firearms before four others grabbed the two men, threw them unceremoniously to the floor and handcuffed them behind their backs. The SOG commander immediately got on the radio to inform the members outside that they had two in custody.

"Before we bring them out, we will do a sweep of the top floor."

Within fifteen minutes, the premises had been thoroughly searched and the SOG team were satisfied that there were no more hostiles inside or around the building. It was then that the handcuffed prisoners were led outside to a position near the Bearcat. They were placed on the ground and searched.

Tony Signorotto breathed a sigh of relief that the situation had been brought to a finish. As he was approaching the SOG Commander, another member of the team came around the front of the building from the rear where he had been involved in the bringing down of Yang Chen. He approached Vince Anderson.

"Sir, from speaking to my offsiders about the sweep they have just done of this place, they didn't find any sign of the drug shipment, but the motor bike Chen was on was carrying a big package of fentanyl."

Anderson looked over at Signorotto and spoke.

"Tony let's just work together to get this sorted. We need

all heads together on this now. Can you call up Max and Kate and we'll have a de brief, please?"

Signorotto nodded and got onto his portable radio and called his Carlton crew up to the Bearcat. When they arrived, he and Anderson had inspected the motor bike that Chen was lying next to. On the back was a box with what the SOG member had described as a package of fentanyl.

Anderson looked at the others and spoke.

"I'll be the first to admit that some of the command structure here, namely myself and unfortunately, Superintendent Reid, who is sitting in her car, have gone about this the wrong way. There will be a lot of repercussions from this raid, but I can guarantee you, none of it will come back on the members at Carlton. I should have insisted Reid listen to your advice, Tony, and I'm truly sorry she didn't. In the meantime though, what are your thoughts on this package of fentanyl. To me it seems like a big enough package but I reckon there has to be more of it, but it's not here in the factory."

Johnny Petran spoke up straight way.

"I've had a look at the motor bike that Chen was riding and I'm thinking that the other ones that shot out of the factory before everything went pear shaped would have been carrying the rest."

"Good thought, Johnny but would Chen have taken the risk on sending out riders if he couldn't get them back. One or more might have decided to shoot through if he had a load of fentanyl that he could offload for a decent price. Chen would have to have been sending them out to a destination or something."

"Where's Chen's phone?" Max chipped in. They all looked at each other until the SOG Commander stepped forward with the evidence bag with the gun and phone that Chen had with him when he was shot dead. Max grabbed it and opened the phone apps.

"There's some sort of tracker on this and it's pinging on the screen."

"There's four different pings and I bet there were trackers on those four motor bikes that came out of here before. They look as though they are in railway car parks. If Chen had got away he would have known exactly where to round up the rest of the fentanyl. We need to get to these locations quick, guys," an excited Johnny Petran said, looking at Anderson and Signorotto.

"Max, go with Kate to two of them and Johnny, you and Mick get to the other two. Go, quick. Max, you take Chen's phone and coordinate everything," Anderson said quickly.

Minutes later, Vince Anderson was standing talking to Tony Signorotto when suddenly, Anne Reid appeared next to them but said nothing.

"I'll explain what we are doing, ma'am," Anderson said as they all stood facing the building, totally oblivious to anything behind them.

"Explain it to a discipline board, Inspector," a stony-faced Reid said standing about two metre from Signorotto with Anderson in between.

Tony Signorotto turned to his right and stared at Reid in disbelief of her attitude. His stare shifted quickly behind her as he saw the pistol being raised towards her back by Bogdan Vulpe who was standing directly behind her.

Tony moved as fast as he could.

But it was never going to be fast enough.

Chapter 52

What happened next would be talked about, discussed, analysed and broken down for a long time to come, not only by members at the Carlton Police station but also around police mess rooms across the state.

As Tony Signorotto threw himself towards Anne Reid in an attempt to push her away from the pistol being aimed at her, he found himself with two choices. The first was never going to work out in time. He couldn't go around Anderson and then shove Reid out of the way. The second was to protect Reid by just throwing himself at Vulpe and by doing so it would hopefully cause the assassin's shot to go astray if he could hit his arm away. He didn't even consider the first option.

Signorotto threw himself at Vulpe but could only attempt to grab the pistol from him. He never had time to draw his own and take aim at the Romanian. Anderson and Reid turned as one as Signorotto moved behind them.

The first of two shots reverberated through the street.

Tony Signorotto fell to the ground, first onto his knees and then slowly toppling forward face down onto the roadway. Anderson reached for his pistol as he stared at Vulpe who was looking blankly down at Signorotto whilst holding his pistol towards his side. The second shot was much louder when it came via the pump action shotgun being held by the SOG Commander.

In what Anderson said later, it all appeared to happen in slow motion. Vulpe was lifted off the ground by the shot and thrown backwards as his legs and arms reached out in front of him. His pistol spun in a parabolic curve and clattered onto the roadway before he landed on his back some two metres from where he had shot Signorotto. He lay in a quickly spreading pool of blood. The last things his mind took in were the burning smell of gunpowder and the sight of a white-faced, shaking Anne Reid standing over him. He tried to speak but he didn't know that his whole lower jaw was missing along with his tongue and teeth. Blood bubbled up from his lungs as a crimson mist descended over him. After two gurgling coughs his eyes closed forever.

The SOG members dragged Reid away from the scene in case there would be another attempt on her life. Anderson, together with Max Tyler and Kate McLaren raced to their comrade as a SOG member radioed urgently for an ambulance.

Signorotto was in a bad way. Vulpe's shot, although intended for Reid had penetrated his gut and even with the stunned Senior Sergeant himself trying to stem the flow of blood by placing both hands over the free flowing wound it was obvious that he needed urgent medical help. Kate McLaren pulled his head onto her lap while Max Tyler ripped off the jumper he was wearing, pulled Tony's hands away and thrust the material over the wound at the same time as pressing firmly down on it. Signorotto tried to speak.

"Reid okay?" was all that came out in a short gasp along with a short flow of blood from his mouth.

Kate McLaren held back tears as she nodded in the affirmative. She screamed at the top of her voice to no one in particular but everyone in general.

"Get a fucking MICA ambulance here now for Christ's sake."

One of the SOG members who was kneeling over Vulpe's body replied that one had been called, but it seemed like hours before they could hear the sound of sirens approaching. Kate held onto her now convulsing boss even tighter than before. She didn't know how long she had been holding him before the two Mica ambulance officers dragged her away so they could work on the injured police officer. Kate didn't know what to do, but she had to vent at someone and it happened like a volcano when she saw the pale form of Anne Reid sitting in the front of a police car staring through the windscreen.

"You should have fucking listened to Tony you stupid bitch. He knows more about policing these fucking streets than you will ever know. This is down to you," she said walking towards the car with the intention of pulling open the door to confront Reid, but as she reached out to grab the door handle and saw the now crying and shaking form of the Superintended she was grabbed around the waist by Max Tyler and dragged away kicking and still screaming obscenities at Reid.

By this stage, another ambulance had arrived and four paramedics were working frantically on Signorotto. Vince Anderson came over to them and looked at one of the frantic ambulance officers without speaking. Words did not have to be said by Anderson.

"He's bleeding badly. Internally it doesn't look good. Bad gut shot. Hate to say it, but you'd better get your Homicide boys down here and not just for the shooter. Your mate here is going downhill quick."

The SOG commander informed Anderson that the Assistant Commissioner Crime was on his way. Reid had been told to stay in the car for the arrival of the detectives. Max Tyler and Kate McLaren stood to one side as an intravenous drip was put into Signorotto's arm and he was lifted onto a stretcher.

"Alfred hospital, you guys," the young ambulance officer said as he raced around to the driver's side.

"I'm going with him in the ambulance, Max," Kate said quickly. "You get onto Susie to meet us at the hospital," she said thinking of Tony's wife.

The ambulance doors closed and it took off with sirens blaring and red and blue lights flashing.

Max Tyler stood looking at the blood-stained ground as he held his blood-soaked jumper.

Christ, there's so much blood, he thought, as the sound of sirens disappeared into the distance.

Chapter 53

Susie Signorotto had basically set up camp in the waiting area of the ICU at the Alfred hospital. Tony had been placed in a medically induced coma to stabilise him and to stop him moving. The bullet that Vulpe had fired had torn a swathe through his intestines and even managed to nick one lung on its' destructive path. Four hours of emergency surgery was now being followed by the never-ending wait. The surgeons had been non-committal about his chances of survival.

There had been a continual stream of friends, well-wishers and close colleagues, some like Jill Norton, the Police Reservist from Carlton who had worked with Tony for years who had stayed at the hospital during two of the nights with Susie only to be relieved during the day by Tony's mother, Sophia. Dom Santino and his wife Maria were a constant with Dom taking no arguments in regard to brining in delicious Italian dinners for any of the ICU staff that wanted them. Kate McLaren and Max Tyler were in and out of the hospital during any of the spare time they had when they could get away from the paperwork and interviews that were being conducted by the Homicide Squad in relation to Tony's shooting, the deaths of Vulpe and Chen and the bikie that Vulpe shot. Experienced members of the Homicide Squad had made their feelings known to the top echelons of the Department about the whole affair. One member had described it as a scene out of the British police movie *London has fallen*, which contained scenes of mass police shootings. Many top members agreed.

One of Tony's closest friends and former colleague, the

now retired Superintendent Phil Stone was more than just an interested and concerned party in the whole affair. In the last month he had been appointed to the Police Disciplinary Board and had been briefed on every aspect not only of the shootings but also on the work practices of Superintendent Anne Reid. On one visit to the hospital he had taken Vince Anderson aside and spoken to him.

"Inspector Anderson, you know that you should have overridden Reid and called a halt to the raid for the drugs. For God's sake man, a phone call to the Crime department would have prevented all this. Going along with her has done your reputation no good at all. For her to put Tony off onto the lookout for Vulpe while you two did overt the factory was stupid. I mean to say, a SOG sanctioned full raid on a factory in a residential street just ended up in a bloodbath with the public looking on. Some of the residents of the street have not only been onto the press but also their local members of Parliament. The Department is copping it in the neck because of the rash decisions you two made. When Signorotto came to you and said that Vulpe had not been caught, the whole operation should have been aborted. Here you two are basically grandstanding while a killer is running around in the same street. Why did you go along with her?"

Anderson could do nothing but apologise over and over.

"Well, we're four days into what is going to be a long inquiry but I can tell you right now that Reid won't be troubled by Vic Pol. The Chief has been in contact with the Metropolitan Police in London and she will be on a plane within days. I think they have only just realised what a single minded, career mad person they sent us. She has been told that she will be stripped of her officer rank not only of Superintendent but also of that of Inspector and has asked to be stationed as a Sergeant back somewhere near where her parents live. That will be her end call as far as they are concerned. Her ego trip days are over as is her career. Remember Inspector Anderson, never rely on someone else to help you with your rise up the ladder when you should know your ambitions are outstripping your capabilities. If Tony pulls through this, and God willing he will, you need to see him face to face and explain why you really just abandoned him for promotion," Stone said as he walked around Anderson and sat outside the door to the ICU alongside of Johnny Petran and Mick York.

"Are you allowed to tell me what happened to the fentanyl shipment even though I'm retired?" Stone said to Petran.

"Technically no, Phil but no one actually leaves '*The Job*' so in answer to your question, the tracker on Chen's phone worked a treat. Between the DRU crews we found the four motor bikes at metro train stations. All of them were neatly packed with what we think is half the fentanyl shipment. The other half was on Chen's bike. We checked with the U/C from the Black Knights and Chi Quang from the Asian Squad and we are as certain as we can be that it is the complete shipment."

"What happened to the undercover member after Vulpe shot his offsider."

"He's back with the Black Knights and has basically told them he took off after the shooting. We are going to organise for him to be arrested at their clubhouse and questioned about why he was with Vulpe. His lawyer will have him zipped up tight by then and we won't chase it too hard. If we don't arrest him and question him the gang will think it's a bit strange as he was a witness to another gang member being shot. There are plans down the track to extricate him from the gang via a so-called fatal accident on his Harley. The Department will help him with a small face job and then he just wants to go trail walking around the world. Kokoda, Machu Pichu, the Camino. After that, who knows."

Phil Stone looked around at the flowers that had been sent to the hospital. Among the many bunches there was one that was a lot bigger than all the rest. He took hold of the tag and read it.

'*From the Chinese Community in Little Bourke Street*'. The flowers were Narcissus, otherwise known as Chinese sacred lilies. They were a sign of good fortune and prosperity. Phil Stone knew exactly who they were from. The Chinese Triad. There was also a large bunch of Peony which had a card attached from the Romanian Consulate. The Peony was the national flower of Romania. The card simply read, A *grateful community*. Phil Stone thought that the Romanian community would have been very grateful for the demise of Bogdan Vulpe.

The flowers that shook Phil Stone though was a bunch of Tudor roses, the national flower of England. Attached to it was a card with no note, just a name. That name was Sir Mark Rowley, the current Chief Constable of the Metropolitan Police in London. Stone saw this as an apology on behalf of the Met Police. It wasn't out of place.

Phil Stone walked quietly out of the ICU with tears in his eyes. He wasn't a religious man but he started to pray.

About the Author

Phil Copsey served with Victoria State Police Force, Australia, for forty years. His hard-earned experience fighting crime on the streets of multicultural Melbourne compelled him to write his true policing books, **Blue Justice**, **The Calibre of Justice**, **The Hand of Justice** and **Killing Justice**. His depictions of characters and crimes are infused with authentic operational details, told through the eyes of his composite character, Sergeant Tony Signorotto. Phil is a natural storyteller who returned to study towards the end of his career to begin his Tony Signorotto crime series.

*

You are welcome to email the author at
philipcopsey@gmail.com

By the same author

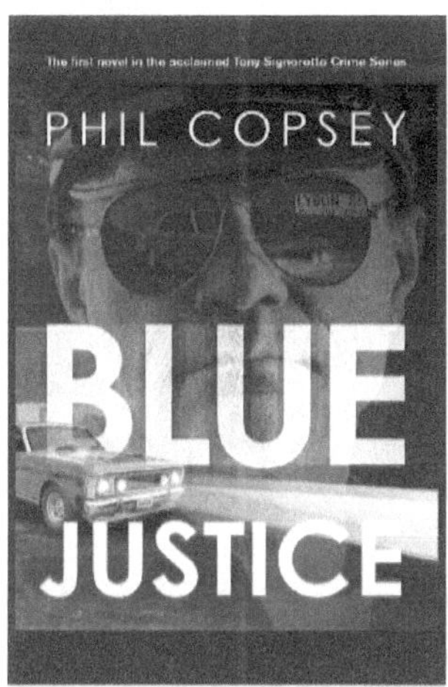

Blue Justice is the first of a gritty new crime series published by in case of emergency press.

Don't look for puzzling cases, corpses in locked rooms, ingenious criminal masterminds, this is a novel about police on the beat: ugly, raw, and morally uncertain. It's not about solving crime. It's about solving problems.

Sergeant Tony Signorotto has good friends, plenty of enemies, and the sort of family connections that just might get him killed.

Buy **Blue Justice** from
https://icoe.com.au/bluejustice.html

The Calibre of Justice continues the story of Tony Signorotto, now newly promoted to the rank of Senior Sergeant, at his beloved Carlton Police Station. Now married to his long-time girlfriend, Tony is looking to extend his career and look after his charter of the safety of the suburb of Carlton in Melbourne's north.

Life should be less complicated. He has made the sacrifice of life on the edge for nine-to-five and the paperwork routine surrounding his mahogany foxhole—until the rumours of a possible firearms raid on the Victoria Police Department. Enough handguns, if stolen, to flood the streets of Carlton and every major city in Australia.

Fast-paced, and brilliantly plotted, The Calibre of Justice is also frighteningly real!

Buy **The Calibre of Justice** from
https://icoe.com.au/thecalibreofjustice.html

The Hand of Justice is an intriguing mix of politics, policing, and power. The stakes are high and reputations will be made or lost.

A new threat has emerged on the streets of Carlton, and it is one of their own in the blue uniform. Do they trust him to see if he can save himself and his career? Or do they give him just enough rope to hang himself?

This thrilling continuation of Phil Copsey's 'Justice' series will take them on a journey that spans illegal gambling, the Russian mafia, an international begging scam, and down a one-way path of murder and kidnapping.

Buy **The Hand of Justice** from
https://icoe.com.au/thehandofjustice.html

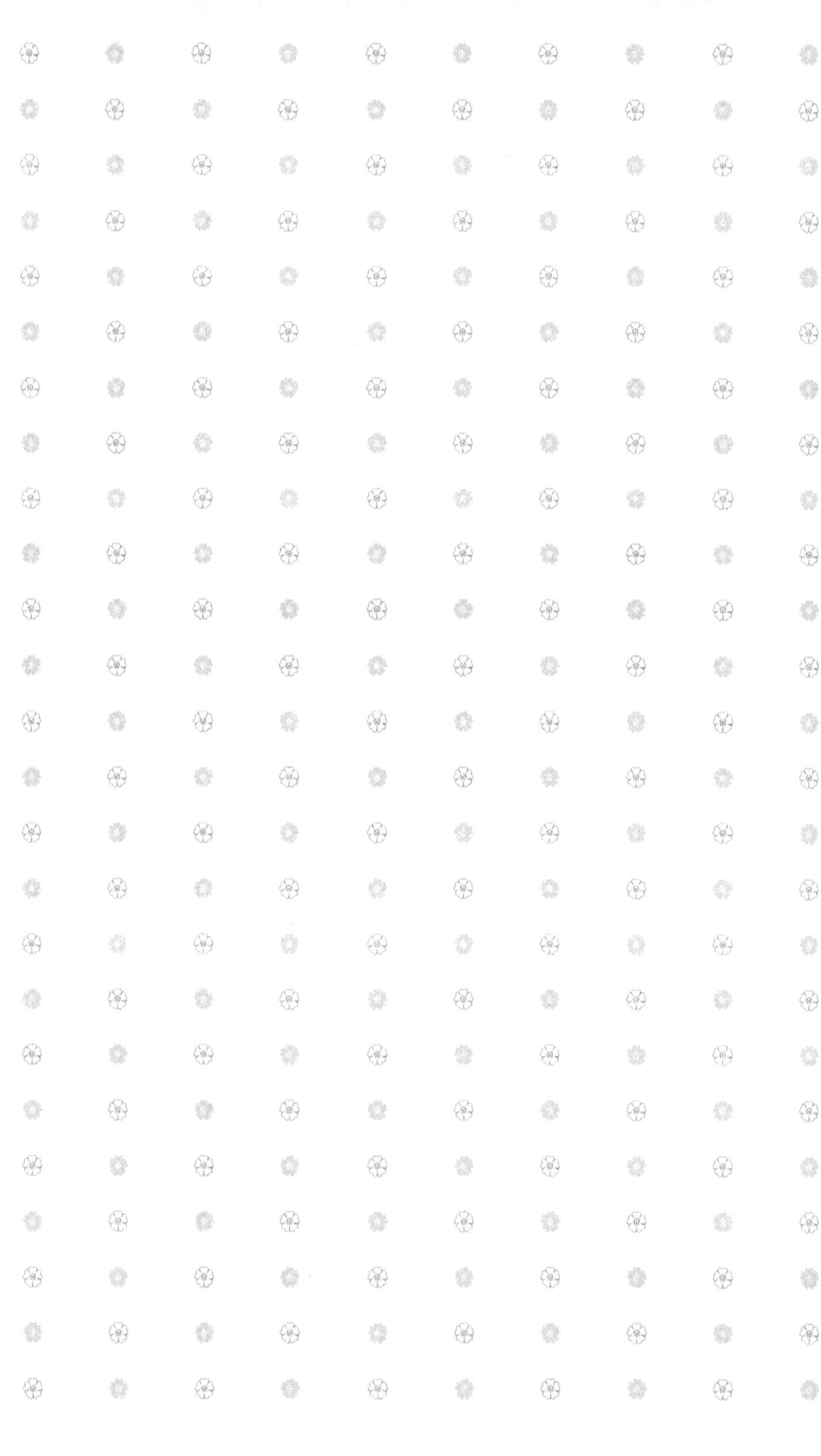

www.ingramcontent.com/pod-product-compliance
Lightning Source LLC
Chambersburg PA
CBHW020507120726
47904CB00003B/729